Take A Shot

Samantha Wayland

Also by Samantha Wayland

Destiny Calls

With Grace

Fair Play (Hat Trick #1)

Two Man Advantage (Hat Trick #2)

End Game (Hat Trick #3)

Crashing the Net

Home & Away

Out of Her League

Checking It Twice

A Merry Little (Hat Trick) Christmas (Hat Trick #4)

Take A Shot

Published by Loch Awe Press
P.O. Box 5481
Wayland, MA 01778

978-1-940839-21-9

Edited by Meghan Miller
Cover Art by Caitlin Fry

This is a work of fiction. Names, characters, places and incidents either are a product of the author imagination or are used fictitiously, and any resemblance to actual persons, living or dead, business establishments, events or locales is entirely coincidental.

Dedication

For my Hearties. I can't begin to thank you enough for everything.

Acknowledgements

I must thank Stephanie Kay, whose superpower appears to be coming up with far better titles for my books than I ever could.

Chapter One

When Tim told the story later, far more often than he cared to, people would comment on how he had such a detailed memory of something that had actually taken a matter of seconds from start to finish. It was as if they thought he couldn't hear the surprise in their tone, or guess the reason for it.

Contrary to popular belief, Tim Robineau was not an idiot. He was perfectly aware he came across as a bit of a doofus sometimes, but it was just because he was super laid back. And liked hanging out with the boys and being stupid.

That didn't mean he was *actually* stupid.

People made a lot of assumptions about hockey players, but more often than not, those assumptions were dead wrong. Everyone admired the quarterback in football, because a good one, a *smart* one, could look out over the field, and the chaos of bodies moving with and against each other, and make the right play.

What people didn't seem to understand was that a hockey team had twenty-two of those guys.

So, maybe that was why Tim remembered exactly how the ice felt under his blades as he swung around behind the net, waiting for the puck. His best friend and roommate, Chris Kimball, was trying to dig the damn thing out of a scrum of players to send it along the boards to Tim. He tapped his stick on the ice, making sure Chris knew he was there, and scanned to see where the rest of the Ice Cats were positioned, looking for whatever the next play would be once he got the puck.

He didn't think anything of the defenseman barreling toward the knot of players hacking at the puck lost among their skate blades and sticks. It wasn't until said defenseman hit the guy on the end—his *own teammate*—that time switched to slow motion.

Every athlete, professional or otherwise, knew the risks. They studied them, learned how to avoid the worst of it and accepted that, if things went sideways, there was only so much they could control. So Tim knew, as he watched all four guys— not one of them less than six feet tall or under a hundred and eighty pounds—topple onto the ice with their legs and sticks tangled, that it wasn't going to end well. He just didn't know who or what would break—or how badly.

The series of noises that followed was crystal clear, in spite of the roar of the crowd that echoed in the rafters: a helmet hitting the ice, a composite stick cracking apart, the dull thud of bodies and pads crashing into each other and the boards. These were familiar. But there was another sound, too. One that Tim had never heard before, but knew was bad even before Chris screamed.

Later, he would learn it was the sound of a healthy twenty-four-year-old man's tibia and fibula being snapped into three pieces. Each.

But even without that knowledge, bile surged into Tim's throat and his feet started moving. He couldn't think of anything, couldn't *do* anything, except obey his gut-deep, visceral need to make Chris stop hurting. It felt like panic and anguish and the Noro virus all at once.

Mike Erdo, the defenseman he'd been planning to pass the puck up to, caught his arm and yanked him to a halt before Tim could grab the player on top of the pile and haul his ass off Chris.

"Think," Mike said sternly, letting go of Tim to drop his stick and shake off his gloves.

Tim did the same and shed his helmet, too, his equipment flying behind him. He was distantly aware of the cold air on his bare fingers and the sweat on the back of his neck. He forgot that though, forgot everything, when his eyes locked with Chris's. He went suddenly numb except for the ache in his chest.

Chris was trapped in the middle of the pile, a man pinned beneath him and another two on top. He stared at Tim, ghost-pale and wide-eyed, his mouth hanging open as if he'd forgotten to close it after he'd screamed.

Teammates shouted for the trainer and gathered around.

More gloves and sticks littered the ice, the sounds of them landing more pronounced for how the crowd had gone eerily silent. The player least entangled with the pile rolled away and was summarily dragged clear.

Hands reached to lift the player on top of the pile. Tim thought vaguely that he should help, that it was what he was going to do, but instead he fell to his knees and yanked off Chris's glove, grabbing hold of his hand. Chris was still staring at him, silent, his expression full of pain and questions. Like Tim could possibly have any answers.

His eyes scanned Chris's body, just for an instant, and he swallowed back another, more violent urge to puke when he saw how Chris's leg was bent.

That was very bad. Very, very bad.

But not as bad as the sound Chris made when they lifted the guy off him.

Chris's face drained of what little color it had left, even his lips going pale. Tears filled his eyes. They looked amazingly blue, his pupils narrowed down to pinpricks, almost swallowed by his irises as he groaned in agony and made a decent bid at breaking Tim's fingers.

It turned out Tim's hand wasn't all that numb after all—not that he cared. He was more concerned by the fact that he was shaking. That they both were. He slid his fingers over Chris's pulse and felt how it galloped under the thin skin of his wrist.

Trainers from both teams fell to their knees, one at Chris's head, the other at his legs, both shouting out orders. They asked Chris questions about being able to move and feel, and all Tim could think was, how was there any doubt that Chris could *feel*?

Whatever answers they derived from Chris's short nods and one head shake were enough. They told Tim to put his free hand under Chris's neck and he did it automatically, without taking his eyes from Chris's. It wasn't until Chris groaned in agony that Tim realized this was the part where they had to lift him off the poor guy who was still pinned beneath him, and straighten that damn leg.

The bones in Tim's hand ground together under Chris's grip, but he held on. Squeezed back. A backboard appeared through the haze of tears now clouding his eyes. Then a doctor and a gurney. And finally they tried pulling Tim away. Chris held on tighter.

"Let them take care of you. It's going to be okay," Tim said.

Chris's grip didn't ease in the slightest. "No."

Tim felt so profoundly relieved to still have Chris's hand in his, he almost smiled.

"Come on," snapped one of the trainers. "If he won't let go, then you're coming with us."

Tim nodded dumbly and skated along beside the gurney. He had the sense to look up at his coach when they got to the mouth of the tunnel that would take them back to the trainer's room.

"Go ahead," Coach said with a grimace. "That was your last shift this period. But be in the locker room in five minutes."

Tim opened his mouth to tell his coach where he could shove it, but a tug on his hand drew him back from the brink of insanity. He looked down at Chris and realized staying to argue would just slow things down. It made the decision easy.

As it turned out, there was little he could do anyway. They didn't even bother going to the trainer's room, rolling straight toward the door being help open by an EMT, the red flashing lights on the ambulance bouncing off the corridor dizzyingly.

Chris closed his eyes and swallowed heavily. When they got to the end of the rubber matting, Tim automatically jerked to a stop before his skate blades could touch concrete.

"Hold up, guys."

"You've got ten seconds," the EMT muttered while he strapped Chris down for travel. A trainer started cutting the laces of Chris's skates. Chris screwed his eyes closed and hissed.

Tim hovered above the gurney and pressed his free hand to Chris's cheek. His friend's eyes snapped open and a tear escaped.

"This is my stop," Tim said, trying to sound calm, but undermined by the croak in his voice. He swept Chris's tear away with his thumb.

Chris blinked up at him. "Come with me?"

"Coach will have my ass if I try it. And I'm pretty sure these guys aren't going to let me into the ambulance with my skates on." As if to prove his point, the trainer thrust Chris's skates into Tim's arms. "I'll come to the hospital as soon as I can," he promised.

Chris's weak smile made the ache in Tim's chest worse.

"It's going to be okay," Tim said with as much conviction as he could muster.

Chris nodded and finally let go of his hand, but Tim could see he didn't believe it. Not as they took him through the door to the waiting ambulance, and not as he looked back from inside it through the little window.

Tim walked back to the locker room on wooden legs, grateful when he pushed through the door and found it still empty. How had the period not ended? It felt like hours had passed since he'd seen Chris go down on the ice.

He recalled that sound—the one he would never forget— and was especially glad the room was clear as he emptied his stomach into the nearest trashcan.

It wasn't just about breaking bones and the kind of pain Tim had never experienced and couldn't imagine. What would happen if Chris couldn't play anymore? Sure, the Moncton Ice Cats were minor league, and Tim and Chris didn't expect to take their hockey careers much further than this, but it was all they had. All they knew. Their friends, their jobs. They'd been in it together since they were practically just kids—eighteen years old and sure they'd died and gone to the heaven where people actually paid them to do what they loved.

Tim wasn't sure how long he stood there, braced against the wall, his head hanging from his shoulders. A warm hand on his neck was the only clue that he was no longer alone. Alexei, their goalie, didn't say anything, just guided him to his seat in front of his locker. After six seasons with the team, this was the quietest intermission Tim could ever remember. No one said anything, not even to ask after Chris, or see how bad Tim thought it was. That alone told him that they all knew exactly how bad it was, too.

For all that Tim would be able to remember every detail of the incident on the ice, he would never be able to recall one damn minute of the third period that followed. He must not have fucked up too badly, since he didn't get his ass chewed out on the bench or afterwards in the locker room as he raced through his shower and getting dressed.

He was just shrugging on his jacket and grabbing his car keys, nodding as guys shouted out messages to be passed along to Chris, when Mike blocked his exit.

Tim was surprised to see Mike was dressed and ready to go. He plucked the car keys from Tim's hand. "You are in no condition to drive."

The hell of it was, Mike was right. Tim wondered distantly how he'd managed to play hockey with his hands shaking like this.

Still, he hesitated. "I'm planning on stopping at the apartment to get some stuff, then staying at the hospital. I won't be able to bring you back here for your car," he told Mike. He had no intention of leaving Chris until he was forced to or could bring him home.

"Alexei will come get me," Mike assured him, putting a hand on Tim's arm. "Come on."

Tim's shoulders slumped. "Yeah, okay. You should drive, then." Another thought occurred to him and he looked up, surprised to find most of the team watching them. "If any of you see Michelle at Smitty's tonight, can you let her know what happened?"

A bunch of the guys nodded, though it was obvious they didn't relish being the ones to tell his girlfriend he was blowing her off. She'd give him one hell of a piece of her mind later, but that was just par for the course. It wouldn't even be the first time she'd accuse him of putting Chris before her and Tim couldn't deal with that shit right now, particularly since she would be right.

Chris woke up, the first time, flat on his back with his head spinning and a complete stranger smiling down at him. He would have cringed if he had control over his body, but he didn't. Somehow, that was less alarming than it should have been.

"Welcome back," the nurse said, smile still in place.

If she said anything after that, he didn't remember it.

When he woke a second time, he was propped up, his head on a nice soft pillow that was doing nothing to help with his pounding headache. He didn't dare open his eyes. He just *knew* that would make it worse. He wished, fervently, to go right back to sleep. But holy shit, it tasted like something had died in his mouth—possibly a small, furry animal. Or maybe he'd swallowed a particularly ripe, unwashed hockey sock.

He swallowed and let out a pathetic noise. A warm hand immediately stroked his cheek and fingers curled around his neck. Something—maybe someone's thumb?—traced over the hinge of his jaw a moment before familiar plastic brushed his lips.

He wanted a sip from that straw, *so much,* but he was teammates with Alexei Belov, so there was no way in hell he was risking it without looking first. Not that Alexei would hit a man while he was down, but most of the team had been conditioned, at this point to the level of Pavlovian instinct, to be cautious.

At first, all Chris could see was dim lights and blobs of darker things. He blinked furiously and the image resolved to Tim hovering over him, his eyes searching Chris's face, brows pinched with concern. That thumb stroked again and Chris had to blink some more, just to be sure he wasn't dreaming.

Had Tim ever touched him like this?

"Here, take a sip. It's water," Tim said, his voice rough and deep and washing over Chris.

Chris tried to do as Tim suggested, fumbling with the straw until Tim held the damn thing in place, his fingers brushing Chris's lips.

If Chris hadn't felt as though he'd just been run over by a Mack truck pulling two trailers full of cement, he might have shivered. All he could manage, though, was a single skipped heartbeat and a sigh of relief as the cold water slid down his throat.

He whined pitifully when Tim took the straw away.

Tim grinned. "You look like a wet cat when you make that face."

Chris scowled at his supposed friend, which only made Tim's grin wider, his handsome face lighting up for a moment.

"The nurse said you could only have a little to start, since the anesthesia might make you feel sick," Tim explained as he set the cup aside on the little tray by the bed. His thick, dark brown hair was standing straight on end. All of it. He looked like a damned hedgehog, which Chris wished his sluggish brain had noticed when he'd been compared to a wet cat. He also looked tired. His full pink lips and thick, arched eyebrows were pulled down in a frown. His eyes, so dark blue people often assumed they were brown, intently focused on the contents of the bedside tray while he arranged it all just so.

Then he turned back to Chris and fussed with the sheets, pulling them higher and smoothing them over his chest.

Chris blinked again, wondering if they'd given him the good shit and he was hallucinating. They'd definitely given him something, since he felt distinctly...detached, and he couldn't feel his leg at all. He wasn't looking forward to when the drugs wore off and that last part changed.

Or the part where Tim, his friend, his buddy—and nothing more, sadly—was fussing over him. He hadn't even known Tim was capable of such...tenderness. If Chris hadn't been as high as a kite, it might have pissed him off to discover something else to love about the guy. It had already been bad enough *before* Tim had apparently stood sentry at his bedside for...hours?

Darting a gaze to the window, he tried to orient himself. It was pitch dark outside.

"What time is it?"

Tim glanced at his watch. "Almost midnight."

"Where am I?"

Tim froze. "You don't know where you are?" he asked, his eyes narrowing.

Chris almost sighed in pleasure when he felt Tim's fingers thread into the hair by his temples, skimming over his scalp. His eyes fluttered closed. He was definitely going to miss this when he sobered up. Or maybe when Tim did. What was his deal tonight, anyway?

"I don't feel any bumps," Tim said, sounding distressed. Chris forced his eyes open again and tried to make sense of the panic on Tim's face. He was having a hard time focusing. "Shit. I didn't think you'd hit your head. Did they go through the concussion protocols?" Tim asked, reaching for the nurse's call button on the mattress. "I'll get the doctor. It's going to be okay, maybe they didn't—"

Chris grabbed Tim's hand, surprising them both, based on Tim's startled gaze.

"I know I'm at the hospital. I meant, am I still in post-op, or did they move me to a room?"

"You're in a room," Tim said, his shoulders coming down from around his ears. "I can't take you home until tomorrow," he added grumpily, smoothing another hand across Chris's chest. "You've been asleep a long time."

Chris let himself wallow in the comfort of Tim's voice. The warmth of his touch. It didn't mean anything, but it was nice to pretend, for just a second. Fuck, these drugs were *great*.

"You should go home. Get some rest," he said eventually, though that was the opposite of what he wanted.

Tim frowned. "I'm not going anywhere."

"But—"

"Shut up."

"Okay," Chris said meekly.

He stared down at the massive lump beneath the covers where his lower leg should be. Not that it wasn't there, but it was kind of weird seeing it when he couldn't feel it at all. He couldn't even feel the gigantic cast they'd already warned him he'd be stuck with for the first week, but he could see the shape of it beneath the blankets. He considered trying to wiggle his leg, but discarded that idea. He'd take this pain-free thing for as long as he could milk it.

After that, everything was going to get a lot harder. Even doped to the gills, he knew that.

He swallowed and looked up at Tim, still hovering beside the bed. Did he plan to just stare at Chris all night? There was a very uncomfortable-looking chair pulled up beside the bed, with a tattered copy of Tim's favorite Neil Gaiman novel hooked over the arm and a duffle bag filled with what looked like both their clothes beside it. There was no way Tim was going to be able to sleep in that damn thing, and they had practice tomorrow.

Well, *Tim* had practice tomorrow. Chris guessed he was done with those, for the time being. Possibly forever.

He let that thought float away and turned his face against the pillow. Tim lurched forward, like he was going to...what?

Chris eyed him warily for a moment, his eyelids already drooping as the day and the drugs caught up with him. A hockey game, an ambulance ride, and the surgery were a lot to take in one afternoon, and that was without the talk with the doctor. The one who said he'd do the best he could, but...

At least they'd been able to pin him back together here in Moncton. He couldn't imagine what the ride from the middle of New Brunswick all the way to Montreal would have been like with his leg in so many pieces.

That thought, for some reason, made him cold. He shivered, almost violently, and wondered if the drugs were doing weird things to his system. Tim resumed his fussing with the covers, as if by tucking them up as close to Chris's armpits as possible, he could make it all better.

Maybe it *did* help a little. There was something that would help even more, though, and Chris was just pathetic and needy enough that he was going to ask for it.

Tomorrow, he'd blame the drugs.

Gritting his teeth, he scooted his butt and his good leg as far over on the bed as he could, careful not to move the other leg at all. Tim put a hand on his hip to try to stop him, but Chris was already pressed up against the railing and settled back on the mattress.

His muscles shook from the exertion. It was incredibly lowering. He was weak and cold and so done with everything at that moment that he couldn't be bothered to care about whether or not he was doing the right thing when he said, "Come here."

Tim looked at him curiously. "Where?"

Chris patted the empty space beside him and closed his eyes. If Tim would rather sleep in the chair, Chris told himself he'd understand. Of course he would. Maybe he'd even get up the energy to ask for another blanket and let himself be soothed by its weight and warmth. But that wasn't what he wanted.

Also, of course, he'd feel bad if Tim ended up pulling an all-nighter because of him. *And* there was the worry of Tim killing them on the way home tomorrow if he fell asleep behind the wheel.

So, really, there were plenty of perfectly good reasons for doing this.

Chris smiled faintly when the mattress dipped beside him. He kept perfectly still, not giving in to the urge to curl into the warmth of Tim's body as he settled onto the bed. Chris opened his eyes at the sound of Tim's sneakers hitting the floor, and watched those freakishly long, skinny feet slid down the bed. As soon as Tim's shoulder pressed against his fully, Chris threw the blankets over Tim's legs.

Tim shut off the lights and Chris turned his head, surprised to find Tim looking back, his face close, his expression unsure. He appeared ready to leap from the bed at the least provocation.

"It's fine," Chris said soothingly, as if it didn't matter. As if he didn't care. "I'm just going to pass out now anyway. You should get some sleep, too."

Tim flashed a quick grin. "Okay."

For a while after that, Chris drifted, not quite asleep, but sort of floating on a cloud of exhaustion and good drugs. When Tim wrapped an arm around his shoulders and pulled him closer, he let himself do what he'd wanted to all along, curling into that warmth as best as he could without moving his leg. Pressing his cheek to Tim's chest, he threw caution to the wind and an arm across Tim's waist.

He smiled, probably dopily, and was glad no one could see his face. Then his thoughts got dimmer still, reality blending with half-formed dreams as he sank deeper into the bed and unconsciousness.

In the morning he would tell himself he had imagined the press of lips to the top of his head and the gentle back-and-forth of fingertips along his arm.

Chapter Two

Tim barely resisted grabbing Chris as he staggered on his crutches, just a few feet shy of his bed. His cast, which reached all the way to mid-thigh, was Ice Cats blue—apparently the doctor was a fan—and gigantic.

"I hate you so much," Chris groaned, shooting Tim a dirty look.

"I know, buddy," Tim said easily, not taking it personally as he restricted himself to steadying his friend with a hand on his back. It had been a long morning of meetings with doctors and convincing the hospital to release Chris. Tim could see the beads of sweat forming on Chris's temples, feel how his muscles shook. As much as the wheelchair to the car had made Chris squawk, it had been a godsend. Sometime around the front foyer of their building, Tim had started to worry he'd have to carry Chris up the stairs to their second-floor apartment, and god knew that would have meant creating a scene, since there was no way Chris was going to go quietly.

Tim pictured himself carrying Chris down the hallway with old Mrs. Boudreaux watching, and grinned.

"Why can't I just sit on the couch, again?" Chris grumbled.

Tim rolled his eyes and pulled one crutch away, helping Chris ease down onto the bed. "Because I have to go to practice in an hour, you're exhausted, you're *high*, and you have the bedroom with a bathroom attached?"

He tried to say it patiently, but since it was the fourth time he was repeating it, he maybe missed the mark some.

Chris scowled and harrumphed, but Tim also noted how he quickly scooted back against the headboard and almost melted into the bed the moment he was settled. Tim would bet anything that Chris would pass out the moment Tim left.

In the meantime, he was pouting mightily, which should not have been as charming as it was.

"Didn't your mother ever tell you that your face can get stuck that way?" Tim asked, turning away to lean the crutches against the wall by the head of the bed and letting himself smile when he knew Chris wouldn't see it.

Schooling his features, he turned back to Chris and pulled all the prescription bottles from his pockets to line them up on the bedside table. He noted how much paler Chris was now than he'd been in the car, and felt another rush of the protectiveness he'd been struggling with since he'd woken up with Chris half on top of him. Not that there was anything wrong with feeling protective. His friend was hurt and needed him. Of course he wanted to help. And Chris was so upset, so tired and *broken* that he'd practically cuddled with Tim all night, drooling on his shirt and clinging to his chest.

Tim hadn't slept much, but what sleep he had gotten had been solid. He figured he would have been up all night in the stupid chair, but being in the bed had meant he would know if Chris needed him, so he'd been able to relax and let himself conk out for a while.

Still, he was pretty tired. So, maybe it was exhaustion that turned that protective urge into something that made him want to run his fingers over Chris's unruly bedhead and tame the wild spikes. That made him want to tuck the sheets in closer, and get the quilt off his own bed, the one his grandmother had made him that was so soft and worn with age that the cotton was silky now.

Because, as previously stated, Tim wasn't stupid. And the burning desire to crawl into bed and pull Chris back onto his chest and spend the day like that? That definitely wasn't bros. Tim didn't know *what* it was, just that it was different. And new. And *weird*.

His cellphone buzzing in his pocket for the zillionth time that morning distracted him from that whole line of thinking, which he definitely wasn't going to pursue. Instead, he looked at the caller ID and sighed. He should probably answer one of Michelle's calls, at some point.

He shoved his phone back in his pocket.

"What do you need?" he asked Chris.

"I'm fine," Chris said, apparently done with pouting and moving on to stoic martyrdom instead. "You should head to the gym before practice."

"Really? So, you're cool with your remote over there on the dresser, and no food and nothing to drink? Instead you'll just subsist on your sadness, maybe?"

Chris narrowed his eyes. "I really hate you."

Tim laughed. "So you keep telling me. Maybe I'll believe you one of these days, but for now, I know you *loooooove* me."

Tim didn't really know what to make of the expression on Chris's face. He turned for the kitchen instead, tossing the remote back over his shoulder as he passed the dresser.

He cringed at the thwack of it hitting...something.

"Hey!" Chris shouted indignantly, but Tim could tell it wasn't real outrage so he kept going. "You could have hit my leg!"

Tim rolled his eyes and shouted back from the hallway, "Quit your bitching. I'm going to slave over a hot stove for you."

"Oh my god," Chris cried. "We're going to die!"

Tim chuckled and refused to comment. Just because he normally didn't like to cook didn't mean he *couldn't.* He was perfectly capable of pulling together something a lot more palatable than anything the hospital cafeteria had on offer.

Which wasn't saying much. Chris's breakfast had looked like the goo people used to sling on Nickelodeon when they were kids.

Unfortunately, his belief that cooking was mostly a waste of time when there were a ton of places close at hand for take-out or delivery meant that the cupboards weren't exactly overflowing with options.

His mother would be appalled by his selections, but he promised himself that he would stop at the store on the way home and make up for it.

Chris looked insultingly shocked when Tim came back into the bedroom with a bowl of Kraft Dinner and a very large smoothie. Tim tried not to act too smug when Chris took the smoothie from his hands eagerly and gulped down a quarter of it.

He also manfully resisted the urge to wipe the smudge of purple from Chris's lips. That would be weird.

"That's perfect. Is it—"

"Banana, blueberry, strawberry, and mango with chocolate protein powder and chia seeds, just the way you like it."

Chris blinked up at him for a moment. He seemed to be doing that a lot. Maybe it was the drugs. "Thank you. It's my favorite."

Tim rolled his eyes. "I know. Why do you think I made it for you, dickface?" He straightened the covers over Chris's legs again, suddenly unsure of what he should do with himself. He needed to get going soon, but he didn't want to leave.

Chris caught his wrist, stopping his movements. "Thank you," he said, looking at Tim in a way that made him feel kind of squirmy. "You should go to practice."

"Yes. Right. Practice." He gestured vaguely over his shoulder toward the door.

Chris nodded, then stared at him as he stood there, not moving. When Chris opened his mouth to say something— probably along the lines of, "What the fuck is your problem?"— Tim jerked into motion.

He didn't get far, stopping again in the doorway. "Call me if you need *anything*."

"I'll be fine."

Tim narrowed his eyes and glared. "Promise."

"Okay, fine, I promise. Now go."

Tim nodded and tried not to let his relief show, then darted into the hallway and ran to grab his bag. He wasn't late, but he was pretty sure that if he didn't get his ass out of the door in the next few seconds, he was never going to leave at all.

And that was just fucked up. Chris was a grown man. He'd be fine. And Tim could call and check on him when he got to the rink. And between drills, too, if he had any concerns.

Maybe at some point in all that, he'd figure out what the fuck was wrong with him.

Chris woke up a few hours later, glad he'd taken the time to eat the macaroni and cheese and drink his entire smoothie before he'd passed out again. As it was, he was hungry, had a terrible taste in his mouth again, and his leg was aching. He checked the time and was relieved to find he could take more of his drugs, wishing they'd kick in faster than he knew they would.

Because while he could ignore his hunger for a while yet, and his need to drink something, the call of nature wasn't going to be put off for very much longer.

He should have asked Tim to help him before he'd left, but he just hadn't been able to bring himself to do it. Tim had already done so much. Dragging Chris's sorry ass to the toilet seemed above-and-beyond the call of duty. And requesting he be left snacks at his bedside was just pathetic.

His cast was huge and heavy, covering his leg from his toes to mid-thigh. But he was a professional athlete, damn it. He could fucking crutch wherever he needed.

Pride was a bitch.

So was falling on his ass in the living room.

He did well standing up by himself, and getting in and out of the bathroom, so he figured he could handle a little change in scenery. He was tired, though, by the time he got to the living room, and when he tried to lower himself onto the couch, he missed the damn thing entirely. He managed to catch himself with his hands and not totally twist up his bad leg, but now he was stuck between the heavy couch and the even heavier, book-filled, coffee table.

He lay there in nothing but his huge fucking cast and his Curious George pajama pants—which Tim had brought to him in the hospital before gleefully cutting off one leg—and wondered what he'd done to deserve this.

Then Tim got home from practice.

"*What the fuck?*"

Chris jerked with surprise, then hissed as the quick movement jostled his leg. He didn't have time to recover, or explain, before two hands were thrust beneath his armpits.

He should have objected, but instead he blinked stupidly, momentarily dumb with awe as Tim's biceps flexed and he lifted Chris right off the floor and planted his ass on the coffee table.

Then Tim stepped back and glared at him, his hands planted on his hips.

"I just wanted to sit on the couch," Chris said, for lack of anything better to say while his heartrate returned to normal.

"You just wanted to sit on the couch," Tim repeated flatly, clearly unimpressed. "And you couldn't have waited for me to get home?"

Chris shrugged. "I wasn't sure when you'd get here," he explained, though it was a sort of a lie since he hadn't even considered it. "You might have gone out after practice."

"I might have gone out after practice," Tim repeated again, now epically unimpressed, if his tone was anything to go by. "If you'd looked at your fucking phone, you moron, you would have known I was coming straight here after you didn't answer it three times."

"Oh, uh, sorry. I was asleep."

Tim's shoulders dropped from around his ears. "I figured, but you still scared the shit out of me."

Before Chris could come up with any response to that, Alexei and Mike appeared in the doorway, which Tim had apparently left open in his rush to save Chris's sorry ass.

"Everybody okay in here?" Mike asked.

"Hey guys," Chris said brightly, hoping even a shred of his dignity was still intact but seriously doubting it. "What are you doing here?"

"They wouldn't let me drive home," Tim muttered.

Chris looked between his friends in confusion.

Alexei explained. "He was freaking out, but still so tired he almost nodded off in the showers anyway. So we brought him home."

Apparently, Chris wasn't the only one with little dignity left.

Perfect.

"Thanks, guys," he said, planting his hand and getting ready to stand. He tried not to let his arm shake, but failed. The surgeon had warned him that the trauma of both the accident and the surgery would throw him off in more ways than just the leg, and he was starting to get the picture. He felt as weak as a baby, goddamn it.

Before he could ask, two sets of hands were lifting him and setting him on his good foot. "Thanks," he repeated, nodding at Tim and Alexei.

He took his crutches from Mike and made his way slowly back toward his bedroom. Fuck, he was tired. All he wanted to do was sleep. Tim darted through the door ahead of him while Alexei and Mike hovered by Chris's side, obviously ready to catch him if he wiped out again.

When he entered his room, Tim was bent over, scooping up the dirty laundry that was scattered across his floor. The moment Chris's ass landed on the mattress, two things happened: His stomach growled loudly, and Tim stood with his arms full of clothing and marched out of the room. A moment later, the sound of the laundry closet doors opening reached them.

"Hungry?" Alexei asked, a small smile on his face while they all listened to Tim muttering about living with slobs who were going to kill themselves by tripping over their own mess.

"Uh, yeah. I'll have to order something, I guess," he said. "There's not much in the house right now."

"I would have stopped at the grocery store on the way home if I hadn't been convinced you were dead!" came Tim's muffled shout.

Mike grinned. "He was very worried."

"He's ridiculous," Chris said loudly enough to be heard down the hall.

Tim stomped past the bedroom door, and the sounds of cabinets being opened and slammed closed again echoed from the kitchen.

"We will go do your shopping," Alexei announced.

"No, I can't ask you to do that. I'll—"

"You'll what?" Tim asked as he stormed back into the room. "Go shopping? Maybe go down the stairs on your face this time?"

He seemed genuinely upset, so Chris swallowed back the instinct to defend his ability to use his crutches. It would have been a lie anyway.

Instead, he watched Tim gather up abandoned shoes and line them up neatly in the closet. He wanted to tell Tim to knock it off, but felt like it wasn't something he should say in front of other people, even good friends.

"We'll be back in an hour," Mike said with another smile. "Do you have a list for the store?"

Tim stood suddenly. "I do. I'll go get it."

Then he was gone again. Chris stared at the empty door. Tim was being weird, even by Tim's standards.

Alexei leaned into his line of sight. "You okay?"

Chris shook his head to clear it. "I'm fine. I have no idea why he's so worked up."

"Maybe, while we're gone," Alexei began, smiling encouragingly, "you two can talk about things?"

"What things?" Chris asked, bewildered.

Mike wandered out of the room, and a moment later Chris could hear him talking to Tim in the kitchen.

Alexei perched on the edge of the bed by Chris's hip. Suddenly this felt like an orchestrated attack.

"Your feelings, maybe?" Alexei suggested gently.

Chris's heart twisted in his chest. "What feelings? There are no feelings. I have no idea what you're talking about." He frowned. "Anyway, he's straight."

Alexei pursed his lips, as though he was trying not to laugh.

"And you're...?"

Chris cringed. "Uh...less than straight? No. Wait. More than just straight, I guess."

Now Alexei did laugh, a loud, joyous sound. "Okay, Chris. Maybe that's what you should tell him, then."

"What would be the point? All it would do is make him uncomfortable," Chris said, his heart pounding. He'd never even considered telling Tim. Ever. How would that even go down?

"Maybe he would like to know."

Chris's racing thoughts jerked to a halt. "You're joking, right?"

"No, I'm not joking."

"We're just friends. I'm his friend. He's not—I can't—it's just like you and Mike. We like each other and spend a lot of time together. We're just like you and Mike. There's nothing more to it," he said, maybe a little desperately.

An alarming sparkle lit Alexei's eyes. "You should probably know that Mike and I are in love, live together, plan to marry, and have a lot of really fucking amazing sex."

"*Oh. That's.*" *Holy shit.* That was a lot to process, and not just the images that were popping into Chris's head. "Uh. Wow. Okay, that's awesome. And ummm...congratulations. On the marriage thing?"

Alexei dipped his chin to acknowledge Chris's lame but genuine response. At some point, Chris would have to do a better job of showing his support, because it was cool his friends had found each other and all that. But none of that was the point right now.

"I'm not going to talk to him," Chris said again, a flutter of panic in his chest when he even thought about it. "I'm happy for you and Mike, but that's just not...*us.*"

"Hmmm." Alexei stood, as if thoughtful and possibly patronizing humming noises were any kind of answer. "Well, then I will be going. We will be back soon."

"Yeah. Okay. Thank you," he babbled, then thought he should

clarify. "For the shopping, I mean. And, you know. For telling me about you guys. I know that's a big deal."

"Yes. And you can tell Tim, but please let us decide who else knows."

"No. Of course. I would never—"

"Chill out."

"Right."

Then Alexei was gone, and Chris collapsed back against his headboard and the pillows piled behind him.

He didn't know how to deal with what Alexei had told him. Let alone what he'd suggested. That was crazy talk. Impossible. Tim wouldn't want to know.

Would he?

Chris took a deep breath and closed his eyes. The trip to the bathroom, the fall in the living room, and Tim's weird behavior had drained Chris's pathetic energy reserves, and now his head throbbed dully while he tried to shut off his whirling brain.

Sleep seemed like a much better option than thinking anyway.

Tim hovered by Chris's bed, trying to decide if he should wake him up or just let him sleep. He still looked pale, which was a mark for letting him rest. He also looked deceptively sweet and young, which Tim should have been taking a picture of to tease him with later, but instead just sort of felt itchy about.

He slid the plates of food onto the bedside table and turned on the light. Chris didn't so much as flinch.

There was no reason Tim couldn't eat his own dinner, at least, but he figured Chris would want company, and eating alone at the kitchen table sounded crappy right now. He would just give Chris a few more minutes to rest before the food got cold.

"What are you doing?" Chris asked in a low, rough voice a few minutes later.

Tim paused in the act of sniffing one of the bottles of cologne on Chris's dresser. "Cleaning?" He quickly lined up the bottle with all the others.

"You're so weird," Chris muttered, running a hand through his hair, which stood up in all directions. It wasn't charming. Really.

"You're just mad because you like living in squalor," Tim said in a superior tone, resorting to an old argument rather than saying anything stupid.

"I hardly think failing to dust and perfectly align the shit on top of my dresser qualifies as squalor, you douchebag."

Tim kept his back to Chris and smiled. "So you say."

There was no response except for the clink of silverware against a plate. "What is this?"

"My mom's Bolognese recipe," Tim said, as if it weren't a big deal.

"You made it?"

"No, I flew my mom in from Toronto."

"Fuck off."

"You fuck off."

Chris sighed, but it sounded more amused than anything else. "Come eat, asshole."

Tim grabbed his plate, scooted around to the other side of the bed, and put it down on the bedside table. Then he stripped off his sweatpants.

"What are you doing?" Chris asked, his voice high.

"What? It's weird to get into bed with clothes on."

Chris looked pointedly down at his pajama pants and t-shirt.

Tim grinned and climbed on the bed. "Yeah, well, you're a prude. Not all of us want to wear more clothes than a nun in church at all times."

"No, *I'm* normal. You, on the other hand, can't seem to keep your clothes on."

That was actually true. Tim preferred to wear as little as possible at any time. But he wasn't going to agree with Chris.

That would just be wrong.

"I left my shirt on, didn't I?" Tim pointed out.

But Chris wasn't listening. Instead he was paused, mid-chew, his mouth full of the dinner Tim had made.

"Oh wow, this is amazing," Chris said with his mouth full, because he was gross. He swallowed and hummed, a sound unlike any Tim had ever heard him make, and promptly shoved another forkful in his mouth.

Tim couldn't look away. When Chris glanced over at him, he quickly dropped his eyes to his plate and took a bite. It *was* pretty fucking good. "Thanks," he said after swallowing, feeling oddly shy about it, for some damn reason.

Chris studied him for a second, and Tim appreciated what a creeper move it had been when he'd done the same thing to Chris.

In a bid to distract them both, Tim reached for the remote and put on the hockey highlights. Montreal had gone down in a ball of flames, *again*, last night. This made Tim unreasonably happy. It wasn't easy being a Toronto fan, so he took his joy where he could find it.

They ate in companionable silence, except to argue about whatever was on the TV. Slowly the nerves that had been grinding at Tim all day started to dissipate.

When they'd finished eating, Tim cleared the plates back out to the kitchen, waving off Chris's objection. "It's not like you would have done it, even if you weren't in a cast."

"Hey!" Chris objected, but it was half-hearted. It was hard to argue with the truth.

When Tim came back, Chris had pulled himself to the edge of the bed, his crutches in hand, and was preparing to stand.

"Dude, what are you doing?"

Chris glared at him balefully. "I have to go to the bathroom. Is that okay with you?"

"No need to be bitchy," Tim said mildly, then helped Chris to his feet. He stayed as close as he could until Chris shut the bathroom door in his face.

Which was fair. Still, he knocked on the door. "If you fall, you better fucking call me for help!"

He couldn't hear Chris's muttered response, but it didn't sound very nice. Tim grinned.

It took about fifteen seconds for Chris to yell through the door. "Go away! I can't go when I know you're hovering outside the door!"

Tim laughed. "Fine, dickface! I'm going to change your sheets, since I'm pretty sure you haven't done it since your mother visited last year."

"Fuck you! And don't change my fucking sheets. They're fine."

Tim ignored him and dug into Chris's closet for his spare sheets, which he eventually found balled up in the back corner. He wondered if they were even clean. Sighing, he went to his own room and got the spare flannel sheets from his closet. And his grandmother's quilt, because he fucking wanted to, okay?

He'd already made the bed and was throwing his quilt over top of the comforter when Chris called for him.

"Tim?" He sounded a little worried.

Tim was at the bathroom door in an instant. "Can I open this?" he asked, his hand on the knob.

"Yeah, go ahead," Chris said. Now he sounded defeated.

Tim opened the door slowly and found Chris leaning against the sink, his shirt off, his pajama pants barely clinging to his bare hips. His pale face and bare chest were covered in a sheen of sweat.

Tim sniffed the air suspiciously. "What have you been doing in here?"

"I wasn't jerking off, you idiot. I was trying to give myself a sponge bath."

Tim grimaced. "Dude, why didn't you just ask for help? You're so fucking stubborn." He grabbed the damp, warm washcloth from the edge of the sink.

"Help? You can't—"

Tim ran the cloth over Chris's shoulders, which shut him up. Tim could feel how the muscles beneath his hands trembled and knew he had to be quick. He wiped over the worst of the sweat on Chris's neck and chest, then wet the washcloth again before gently wiping Chris's face.

He didn't like how dazed Chris looked by the time he was done.

"There, that's going to have to do for now. You look like you're about to fall over."

Chris's eyes focused into a glare. "This fucking cast is heavy, and I'm not supposed to let it touch the floor, let alone put any weight on it."

"I *know*, which is why you're meant to ask for *help*."

Rather than argue, Chris straightened and hopped toward his crutches.

"Oh for Christ's sake," Tim said, handing them to him. "Can you even make it back to bed?"

Chris took a deep breath and nodded, which wasn't very convincing, but Tim held his tongue and stayed close while Chris made slow progress. As soon as he turned his back to the bed, Tim grabbed Chris's arm to help him sit on the bed without collapsing.

Chris ran a hand over his pillow. "Are these your sheets?"

"Yes, Pigpen. I thought the flannel might be nice."

Chris looked at him oddly. "Thanks."

Tim shrugged and mumbled, "You're welcome," while he helped Chris get settled back on the bed.

When he reached for Chris's pain meds, Chris stopped him. "Can you get the ibuprofen from the bathroom? I don't want to take that stuff anymore. I'm tired of feeling so out of it."

Tim frowned and checked to see how much color had come back to Chris's face. Not enough. "Just take the good stuff tonight, so you can sleep, okay? Then switch in the morning."

"Why do you even care?" Chris asked, clearly exasperated.

"Because I do," Tim snapped, for lack of a better answer. He was still trying to figure out what the hell was going with all these weird feelings he was mostly trying to ignore.

Self-awareness: not his thing.

"Also," he added, "you need to sleep so you can heal. So, whatever, shut up and take the drugs."

Chris did, but not without a lot of disgruntled looks.

Tim waited until Chris was settled back again before switching off all but one dim light and turning the TV volume down. "I'm going to go clean up the kitchen. Shout if you need anything, okay?"

"Yeah. Sure," Chris said, sounding defeated again.

Tim didn't know how to fix that, but he seriously hated it. He squeezed Chris's shoulder once before leaving him gazing vaguely at the TV. When he came back twenty minutes later, Chris was out cold, still sitting up in bed.

Tim shook Chris's shoulder to rouse him only long enough to help him scoot down on the bed. As soon as his head hit the pillows, he was out. He was still way too fucking pale for Tim's comfort, but hopefully sleep would help.

Sighing, Tim stripped out of his t-shirt and climbed in the other side of the bed, switching off the light and curling up facing away from Chris.

He didn't consider going back to his room. If he did, he just *knew* Chris would try to get up in the middle of the night without asking for help. This way, he'd be close enough to know when Chris was awake and could step in before he tried to do anything stupid.

Really, Tim was a great fucking friend for being there, and he intended to point that out when Chris squawked about it in the morning.

He snuggled down into the bed further, enjoying the fresh, soft sheets already warmed by Chris's body just a foot away. His grandmother's quilt was familiar beneath his fingertips, as comforting as the soft sound of Chris's breathing behind him.

Chapter Three

Chris woke up from a strange dream about being locked in a sauna to find himself pinned to the bed by Tim. Jesus Christ, the guy was a fucking blast furnace.

Maybe it was the drugs, or the exhaustion of the past few days, or his subconscious getting the best of him, but for five minutes, he just lay there and enjoyed the hell out of it. Tim was curled around Chris, his breath tickling the back of Chris's neck, his arm tight around Chris's ribs, a wide palm pressed over his heart.

Chris had a vague memory of waking up sometime in the middle of the night, his back aching from having been flat out on it for most of the day. He'd carefully rolled over, trying and failing to find a way to sleep comfortably on his side until Tim had tucked a pillow between his knees. Chris couldn't remember where he'd thought Tim had materialized from at that moment, but now it made sense. In hindsight, he was grateful for the help, but even more grateful for the good drugs, since he wouldn't have been able to sleep another wink if he'd been aware that Tim was *in bed with him.*

Instead, he'd passed out and apparently rolled partially onto his front, his good leg bent onto the mattress, and Tim's stretched along behind it, resting on his cast and the pillow.

Chris shifted carefully and reached behind him until his hand encountered a bare hip. For one hysterical moment, he thought Tim might be naked—he totally wouldn't put it past him, the fucking nudist—but then his fingers brushed against Tim's boxer briefs.

Tim grunted in his sleep, his hips shifting closer to Chris's ass, his hold tightening. Chris held his breath and tucked his hand back onto the bed in front of him.

He really didn't want Tim to wake up. Not yet. Not when the wriggle of Tim's hips had sent a shot of arousal straight to Chris's morning wood.

What the fuck was he supposed to do now?

If it wasn't for the fucking cast, he could have rolled right out of the bed and gone straight to the bathroom, maybe using some careful hand placement to conceal whatever was going on in his pajama pants that shouldn't be. But the cast, and the crutches, weren't going to allow him to dash anywhere. And they sure as shit weren't going to let him hide *anything*.

Chris attempted to very, very subtly shift his hips to ease the pressure against his dick.

Tim hummed, his lips pressing against Chris's neck, and wriggled closer.

Chris closed his eyes and took a series of deep breaths. His erection needed to *go away.* Jerking off was definitely not an option, even if it would only take about a minute at this point. Instead, he thought about his next doctor's appointment in a few days, then about his last family reunion and how awful his Aunt Debbie had been, pinching his cheeks and asking about a girlfriend. He even tried to picture the Vancouver winning the Stanley Cup.

The last one almost worked.

Chris sighed and accepted he was going to have to lie there and wait it out. He hadn't spent this much time worrying about a boner since he'd been in middle school, and felt fucking ridiculous about it. Tim must have sensed something in his sleep, because his hand started rubbing Chris's chest, his lips pressing more firmly to the back of his neck.

And that didn't help *at all.*

There was nothing Chris wanted to do more than lean back against the pressure of those lips. To have them moving across his skin. To feel that hockey-roughened palm glide down his belly and sneak beneath the waistband of his pajama pants.

Now Chris had no choice but to thrust his own hand into his pants—and not for any fun reason, either. His dick was bent in half in there, and if Tim was going to keep torturing him, Chris had to do something or risk injury.

Of course, *that* woke Tim up.

Chris half expected Tim to leap out of the bed when he realized they were spooned tightly together. Or at least move swiftly to the other side of the mattress. Instead he yawned and rubbed the tip of his nose along Chris's nape. Chris jerked his hand from his pants before the temptation became too great.

"You okay?" Tim asked, his voice rough with sleep and unfairly sexy. He propped himself up on his elbow and watched curiously as Chris pulled his arm from beneath himself.

"Sure," Chris said quickly, his voice stupidly high and the dead opposite of sexy. "My arm. It...uh...fell asleep."

"Oh, sorry," Tim said, rolling away a little. Chris instantly felt cold, but was relieved that he might actually get out of this without embarrassing himself. Then Tim pulled at his shoulder. "Here, roll onto your back and get your weight off that arm."

"No! I mean, that's okay. It feels better now."

"Come on, you need to move if you want to get feeling back," Tim said, throwing the covers off so he could help Chris get his good leg up and over the cast and back onto the mattress.

Chris didn't have much choice but to go along, trying to be casual about the whole thing as he landed with his shoulders to the mattress and glanced down at himself.

Yeah, it was pretty obvious what was going on down there. Tim had stopped moving, his hand still wrapped around Chris's good knee, his eyes on the tent in Chris's pants.

Which was just *awesome.* Finally, his boner found a reason to retreat.

Chris was trying to figure out if he should apologize, or ignore it, or what when Tim's phone buzzed on the table on the far side of the bed. The second Tim turned away to grab it, Chris sat up and yanked the covers back up to his waist.

"Hello?"

Chris didn't have to be a genius to know who was on the other end of the phone. Even if he hadn't been able to hear the tinny screeching coming from the earpiece, he would have known by Tim's cringe and his expression as he listened to Michelle chew him out. It was, sadly, a familiar look.

Tim was a really great guy. He was smart and funny and caring. But he had the *worst* taste in girlfriends. Not that they weren't also nice and smart and funny. But somehow they could be all those things and still be totally wrong for Tim. Finding these women was like Tim's superpower or something.

Tim tried to get a word in edgewise, but clearly Michelle wasn't having it. Smiling apologetically at Chris, Tim climbed from the bed and wandered toward the bathroom. Chris stared at the flex of muscles across Tim's broad, bare back. The full length of his long, strong thighs exposed where his underwear had ridden up while they'd been, apparently, cuddling most of the night.

Tim pulled the phone from his ear and hit a couple buttons on the screen. Suddenly Michelle's voice was loud in the room.

"...the fuck you were thinking. I showed up at Smitty's and your teammates, who all looked embarrassed, by the way, are the ones telling me that you're not going to show!"

Chris cringed, but Tim just shrugged, sanguine as ever in the face of an infuriated woman. "It will take her a while to wind down," Tim said, putting the phone down on the dresser. Chris looked at him in horror, gesturing at the phone. "Oh, no, I muted our side. I gotta pee."

And with that, he left Chris listening to his girlfriend's tirade while he slipped into the bathroom and took a freaking leak with the door open. Chris flopped down on the bed and ground the heels of his palms into his eye sockets, because he really didn't need to see that. Too bad blinding himself didn't keep him from listening to something he couldn't possibly ignore but really shouldn't be hearing.

Apparently, Tim never did romantic things. He didn't use endearments, and all he wanted to do was hang out with his friends. Sometimes a woman wants more than a beer out with the guys...and so on. Chris had heard most of this before, at various points over the years, hollered at Tim by any number of women.

And he supposed he understood their position, truth be told. But at the same time, all Chris ever wanted to do was hang out with Tim and their friends and have a beer, so it was hard to be totally sympathetic.

He yanked his hands away from his face when Michelle said, "You know what? I don't care that you fuck like a pile driver crossed with a fucking contortionist! It's not worth it. You never put us first. Put *me* first. So what if you've got a big dick and talented tongue? I can't believe I let you fuck me on the hood of my car, and that ice cube trick was hot, but…"

Tim was now madly trying to finish up in the bathroom. Any other man on earth would have skipped washing his hands, but neat-freak Tim couldn't, so Chris was treated to a litany of sexual escapades. He couldn't help but laugh, turning to bury his face in the pillows. How was this even his life? He was a little horrified with himself when his dick got back in the game. But seriously, Tim could fuck for *hours*? Chris really hadn't needed to know that.

Finally Tim dove from the bathroom and scooped up his phone and took it off speaker, almost dropping it in his haste.

"Michelle!" he said loudly, and the noise stopped. "What are you trying to say?"

Chris knew the answer to that question even without the phone on speaker. Apparently, Tim wasn't surprised either, though he did jerk the phone away from his ear and stare down at it, his expression bewildered. "She hung up on me."

Chris barely controlled the urge to roll his eyes.

"And she dumped me."

"I'm sorry."

Tim sighed, his shoulders bent. "No, you're not."

"What?" Chris said, sitting up again. "Of course I am."

"You hated Michelle."

"No, I didn't! I thought she was nice."

"You barely spoke to her."

Was there a nice way to tell his friend he'd long ago stopped trying to be friends with his girlfriends, since they never lasted more than three months and most ended up hating him with a fire that burned hotter than a thousand suns?

Nope.

"I'm sorry. I hope I didn't cause problems for you with her. I didn't mean to be...distant, or whatever."

Tim gave him a look. "I don't get you."

"What does that mean?" And when did this become a conversation about him?

"You're always so..." Tim waved his hand vaguely, obviously searching for the right word. "...*reserved*!" It didn't sound like a compliment.

"I am not."

"You are. I asked you months ago what you thought of Michelle and you said she was nice."

"She was nice! I mean, she is nice, I guess. Just maybe not to you. Today." Chris shut his mouth before he could dig that hole any deeper.

"You didn't think she was nice." When Chris opened his mouth to object, Tim held up a hand. "Okay, you did. But I could tell you were thinking a lot of other things about her, too, and you didn't say any of them."

"It wasn't my business."

"You're my best friend! And I *asked*. How is that not your business?"

"I'm not as good as you are at talking about what I'm feeling, okay? I like to keep some things to myself."

"Why? Don't you think I'll understand? I trust you. You can tell me anything."

Chris scoffed at that, because seriously.

"Holy shit, *you* don't trust *me*. That's it, isn't it?"

Chris looked at Tim, alarmed. "No! Of course that's not it. I trust you more than anyone."

"Right," Tim said shortly, coming around the bed to scoop his clothes off the floor, clearly intending to leave the room.

Chris panicked. He didn't want the conversation to end this way, and he was in no condition to chase after Tim. He rolled across the bed, dragging his bad leg behind him, and grabbed Tim's arm.

Tim looked down at him with the blankest expression Chris had ever seen on his expressive, couldn't-hide-a-thing face.

"I trust you," Chris said, his voice almost cracking, his grip on Tim's arm fierce.

"Then tell me what you're thinking. Right now. Don't be reserved or whatever. Just *say* it."

Chris let go of Tim's arm and sat back, using the excuse of rearranging his legs to give himself some time. He glanced up at Tim and his terrible, blank expression. Chris *hated it.*

"They don't deserve you," he said at last, shocking even himself.

"Who? Michelle?"

"Any of them. Any of the women you've dated and who have dumped you."

"Why not?"

"Because you're always yourself with them, and they don't appreciate that enough."

Tim sat on the edge of the bed and dropped his clothes back into a heap on the floor. He didn't look blank anymore. He looked *bleak.* "I try to be, but I don't know. Maybe I shouldn't be. I mean, look at my track record. I must be doing something wrong."

Chris reached out, but caught himself at the last second and let his hand fall back to the bed. "You're not doing anything wrong, Tim."

"Yeah, well, that's not what I've been told. All I want to do is hang out with the guys. My friends. You. That's me being myself, and apparently that's not okay."

"But it *is.*"

"And I like talking about hockey, but that's not interesting, I guess."

"Sure it is."

"God knows women never think the pranks are funny. And I'm not even the one pulling them!"

Chris chuckled. "Yeah, that's true. Granted, sometimes your girlfriends have gotten caught in the crossfire on those."

Tim sighed. "Tina refused to ever speak to me again after the hair-removal cream incident."

"No, I imagine she was upset, what with having to get a wig and all."

Tim's lips twitched. "It was kind of funny, though."

Chris grinned. "I thought so. I mean, not the Tina part, but who knew you had such a lumpy head, dude?"

Tim laughed, but the sound died off quickly, his smile sliding away. "I'm doomed, aren't I?"

"You're not doomed."

"I'm never going to find someone who loves to hang out with the guys."

"Yes, you will."

"And who doesn't care that they're actually a bunch of idiots and pranksters."

"Sure."

"And won't care that I travel half the year, and work a ton of nights when I'm home. Who wants to talk about hockey as much as I do. Who's happy going out for a beer and some steak and then coming home to chill out, because I'm too fucking tired in the middle of the season to go out and party. Who the hell is going to put up with that? Let's face it—I'm fucked."

"No, you—" Chris sighed and closed his mouth. What could he say? Tim could be a total pain in the ass, but he was perfect in all the ways that mattered to Chris.

"You have your reserved face on again," Tim muttered darkly. "What aren't you telling me?"

"Nothing."

The blank expression was gone. And the bleak one. Now Tim was *pissed*. He shot to his feet. "You know what, I'm done. I'm pouring my heart out here, and you can't even tell me the truth. Just say it! You think I'm fucked, too. Admit it."

"That's not what I was thinking at all."

"Then *what*?" Tim shouted, furious.

Something in Chris snapped. In all the years they'd known each other, *this* was what made Tim so angry he yelled at Chris for the very first time? Fuck that. If he wanted to know Chris's inner-most thoughts so badly, then he could deal with the fallout.

"That person does exist!" Chris shouted back. "There already *is* someone who loves to spend time with you, who loves hockey and your friends and their ridiculous pranks. Who gets that you have to travel and that you're tired!"

Tim blinked, appearing utterly bewildered. "Who?"

"Me, you asshole! *Me*."

Tim threw his hands in the air. "What about you?"

"*I* appreciate you exactly as you are. I love our life. Our friends. *You*. Even the super fucking irritating things, because apparently there is something wrong with me. I love that you can't hide what you're feeling, almost ever. And that you say what you're thinking, even when I can't do the same. I like living with you, a fucking neat-freak nudist, *and* working with you, and there's never been a time, not once, that I was tired of being around you. You're gorgeous and you're kind and you're the best person I know. So shut up about there not being someone who can appreciate everything about you. There already is. And unfortunately for you, it's *me*."

Tim stared at him, his eyes so wide they were practically bugging out and his mouth hanging open. It wasn't his best look.

Chris's heart was pounding so hard, he could feel it in his face. His fingers. He watched Tim warily, waiting for some reaction other than shock. He couldn't decide if he should be relieved or terrified when Tim slowly sat down on the bed beside him. The silence stretched until Chris couldn't stand it anymore.

"Look, I get that I'm not what you're looking for. I'm sorry if this makes things weird. Actually, I'll never forgive myself if this makes things weird. At least Alexei will be proud of me, I guess," he said nonsensically, with a small, sad smile. "He and Mike are together, by the way. Apparently they fuck like bunnies. So, yeah, good for them. But don't say anything to anyone else about it, okay?"

"Okay." And that might be the meekest word Chris had ever heard Tim speak, but at least he'd finally said *something*.

"Right. So, I had no idea. But it's cool they decided to confide in us," Chris said lamely, not sure how else to fill the silence.

"No," Tim mumbled.

Chris wasn't even sure what part Tim was responding to. He finally risked a glance up. "It's not cool?"

Now Tim looked offended. "Of course it is!"

"But you just—"

"Shut up. I'm thinking."

"Don't hurt yourself," Chris snapped back automatically.

Tim smiled. A huge grin that took over his entire face. Chris's speeding pulse skipped a beat.

"You really mean it," Tim said, like he'd just started to believe it instead of Chris maybe having decided to have a big awkward moment of super gayness for shits and giggles.

"Of course I mean it, you fucking mmmph—"

Tim's lips crashed onto his, stealing his words and his breath and knocking him back against the pillows. Chris flailed his hands in the air, useless, as he tried to process that fact that Tim was *kissing him.*

How could this be happening? This wasn't supposed to happen. Chris was never going to tell Tim how he felt and Tim was never, ever supposed to touch his lips to Chris's. To thread a hand into Chris's hair and nip at his lower lip. Tim shouldn't hum like this, a pleased murmur pressed into Chris's lips.

But it was good. It was so, *so* fucking *good.*

Chris finally knew what to do with his hands. He dug his

fingers into Tim's broad, muscled shoulders and pulled him closer, holding on for dear life. The moment Tim's tongue touched his lips, he opened to it, meeting it with his own and drowning in Tim's kiss.

Chris had heard of the whole fireworks-going-off thing, and maybe he'd thought angels would sing if he ever kissed Tim, since it had to be some kind of fucking miracle, but he'd never once thought the sound that would accompany this moment would be a goal horn.

And yet, it was fitting.

He whimpered when Tim tore his mouth away and immediately reached for his... phone?

"Shit," Tim whispered viciously.

The fog cleared from Chris's brain enough for him to recall that Tim's alarm on his phone was, in fact, a goal horn. Which maybe made a little more sense than the whole choir-of-angels thing.

"How long do you have?" Chris asked, trying to act normal when he kind of felt like hiding under the covers and also maybe tackling Tim to the nearest flat surface.

"Five minutes." Tim jumped to his feet, grabbed his clothes, and ran for the door.

"You set our alarm to wake you up *five minutes* before you have to leave for practice?" Chris shouted out the door at Tim's back.

He couldn't quite make out Tim's response, but he got the gist of it.

"Fuck you, too!" he replied.

Tim reappeared in the doorway, already dressed and hopping around on one foot to put on his other shoe. "We'll talk about that when I get home."

And then he was gone.

"Hey, Robineau! You planning on joining us anytime soon?"

Tim's head snapped up, his cheeks burning when he realized

the entire team had stopped mid-drill to stare at him while he was drifting around in the corner, lost in thought.

"Sorry, Coach!" he called, skating back to the line and trying to keep his mind on what he was supposed to be doing, and not letting it drift back to Chris lying in his nice, warm bed at home. Never in his life had he been less engaged in what was going on around him while on the ice. Not even when Chris had been in the hospital. Then he'd just been numb, his brain focused entirely on hockey.

Today his brain was definitely not numb. More like on fire. As were a few other body parts, though his protective gear was doing a pretty good job of keeping that under control.

"Hey, you okay?" Mike asked when he skated up to get in line.

"Yeah, sure," Tim said. "Just distracted."

Distracted seemed like a tame word compared to whatever the hell he was. His mind was blown. *I kissed Chris.* A dude. His best friend. He couldn't even remember deciding to do it. It just struck him as a good idea and he'd gone for it. An experiment gone wildly *right.*

So yes, he was *distracted.*

He looked back at Mike to see him making eye contact with Alexei. They seemed to be having an entire conversation with their eyebrows alone.

"Hey," he said quietly, waiting until Mike's attention was back on him. "I'm happy for you."

"What?" Mike appeared mildly alarmed.

"Chris told me. Alexei told him, apparently."

"He did?" Mike looked at Alexei as a slow smile grew on his face. "That's...cool. Thanks."

Tim wondered how he hadn't guessed about Mike and Alexei when it was readily apparent they couldn't keep their eyes off each other, and that wasn't anything new. Alexei was coming towards them, a big, happy smile on his face.

"Look, can I ask you something?"

"Sure," Mike said, though his eyes were still glued to Alexei.

Tim waited until Alexei joined them before dropping his voice and asking, "Did you know Chris had a thing for me?"

Tim cringed when Mike and Alexei turned to him with the exact same expression on their faces. He knew this look, too well. It was the same one he always got when people thought he was being exceptionally dumb.

Coach saved him from having to say anything when he shouted, "Okay, ladies. Three-on-three drills next! Save the gossip for the locker room—preferably when I'm not anywhere nearby."

Mike smiled at Tim. "Do you really need us to answer that?"

"Guess not," Tim mumbled. "I've been an idiot, haven't I?"

"Just a little clueless," Mike offered gently.

"What matters now," Alexei said, "is what you're going to do about it."

Which was funny, since that should have been the big issue—but it wasn't. Sometime between leaving the apartment and arriving at the arena, Tim had realized a few things. One, he was an idiot. Two, kissing Chris had been super hot. And three, he wanted to do it again. A lot.

It was scary as hell, but Tim would be damned if he was going to let that stop him. Nobody was or had ever been as important to him as Chris. That meant something.

And Tim was determined to figure out what.

That was what he was going to do about it.

Chapter Four

Two hours later, Tim threw the door to their apartment open with a flourish. "Honey, I'm home!"

It was an old joke, but as he toed off his shoes in the front hall, it occurred to him that it suddenly had a different meaning. Maybe. Did it?

This shit was confusing.

Also, why the fuck hadn't Chris answered?

Tim double-timed it to Chris's room, his heart stopping when he found the bed empty. "Chris?"

"In here."

Tim clapped a hand on his chest and turned toward the bathroom. Chris hadn't left. Of fucking course he hadn't left. He could barely move. And he wouldn't do that. Even if he was freaking out about what had happened this morning.

Tim pressed his other hand to the bathroom door. "You okay in there?"

"Kind of?"

"What the fuck does that mean?"

"Just get the fuck in here. You know you want to come save my sorry ass again."

So, Chris was definitely in a snit about something. Tim opened the door slowly, both because he didn't want to knock Chris over and because he was worried about projectiles aimed at his head.

He found Chris sitting on the toilet lid, a towel spread out beneath him, another over his lap. Other than that, and his cast, he was completely naked. The shower was on and billowing steam into the sweltering room.

"Uh? What the fuck are you doing?" Tim asked curiously.

Chris let out a huge sigh and tossed a washcloth back into

the sink. "I was trying to get clean. I feel disgusting."

"Okay," Tim said with a smile, closing the door behind him to keep the heat in. "So, what's the plan? Get in the shower and melt your cast off?"

"Shut up. I was cold."

Tim could see the goosebumps across Chris's shoulders, just from having the door open for a minute. He traced his fingers over them and Chris shuddered. Tim was pretty sure that *wasn't* from being cold, and the thought sent a surge of heat through him.

"How about I help you again?" Tim asked, tugging off his own shirt, which was already plastered to his skin.

"Uh, what?" Chris asked, staring at his chest.

Tim didn't flex. He didn't. But it was close.

Instead, he pushed his sweats to the floor and kicked them away, leaving him in only his boxer briefs, his dick pushing forward.

Chris ran his eyes down Tim's body.

"Like what you see?" he asked, curious.

"Yes," Chris croaked.

"But you see it every day. Isn't it sort of...I don't know, the usual?"

Chris stared pointedly at the growing bulge in Tim's briefs. "This is different."

Tim smiled and knelt between Chris's knees, careful not to bump the cast as he put his hands high on Chris's thighs and rubbed. "How about I help you with your bath?"

"Uh, what?"

"Let's get you clean," Tim said, as innocently as he could manage as he reached for the washcloth and turned on the sink. "I promise to do a more thorough job this time."

"But. You can't—I already—" Chris's voice choked off when Tim ran the cloth down Chris's chest, and around his ribs.

"Good," Tim murmured, watching his hand run over Chris's

skin, the washcloth leaving a shiny trail as he rubbed it over Chris's pecs and lower. Chris's stomach jerked against Tim's hand, and he glanced up to see Chris watching him with a wide, uncertain gaze.

With his hand hovering just an inch over the towel in Chris's lap, Tim changed direction and curled his arm around Chris's waist, focusing on trailing long swipes down Chris's back for a while. He had to lean in to reach, his nose brushing the shell of Chris's ear as he made sure he hit every spot. He ended by following the trench of Chris's spine all the way from the nape of his neck to the swell of his ass.

Chris's breath stuttered in Tim's ear when Tim tucked the washcloth and his fingers into the very top of the crease of his ass and wriggled.

"Jesus Christ," Chris muttered weakly.

Tim sat back. "Feel cleaner now?"

"Um, what? Yes?"

"Great. We're almost done." Tim tried not to grin at the befuddled look on Chris's face.

"Almost?"

"Don't want to miss any spots," Tim promised before hooking his fingers in the edge of the towel still modestly draped over Chris's lap and tugging.

Chris's hands jerked, like he might make a grab for it, but he clenched them into fists at the last moment and pressed them to the sides of his thighs as Tim dragged the towel off and dropped it onto the floor.

Chris's bravery was almost as sexy as the sight of him completely naked. Tim stared at Chris's cock, fully erect and pressed to his belly now that the towel wasn't holding it down.

This was definitely *different*. And not just because Chris was unusually modest for a guy who spent so much time in locker rooms. Tim had seen literally *hundreds* of naked men in his life, and not one of them had made his pulse speed up, or his skin prickle with awareness and the need to touch.

Tim took his time rewetting the washcloth, trying to take it all in and settle himself down, then slid back until he was between Chris's feet. Chris giggled when Tim began to clean the toes poking out from his cast.

"What are you doing?"

"Dude, I'm the one who's constantly picking up your smelly-ass socks. I know how bad your feet get."

"Oh," Chris murmured as Tim ran the tip of his finger along the tender undersides of each toe. "I'm sorry."

"It's cool. I get that I like things neater than you."

"I like them neat, too. I just…"

Either Chris didn't have an explanation or he'd lost his train of thought when Tim rubbed the bottom of his good foot with the warm washcloth. Did Chris have a thing about his feet?

Curious, Tim lifted the freshly washed foot and sucked the big toe into his mouth.

"Oh, *fuck.*" Chris groaned, his cock jerking against his belly.

Yep. Definitely had a thing about his feet.

Chris's hand jerked toward his dick, but Tim caught him by the wrist and watched, mesmerized, as a pearl of precome formed on the tip of Chris's cock and then ran down one side.

He pulled Chris's toe from his lips with a pop. "Do you have a foot fetish?"

"As of fifteen seconds ago, apparently," Chris admitted ruefully.

Tim smiled and focused on washing Chris's good leg, paying extra attention to the skin behind his knee and the smooth, remarkably hairless expanse of his inner thigh. Tim had about a hundred times more hair on his body than Chris, which he already knew from years spent in the locker room together. Hell, Chris still couldn't grow a playoff beard that wasn't worth hours of mocking, which was *great*. But Tim was still surprised that this skin was so smooth. So soft.

Chris let out a strangled groan when Tim ran the backs of his fingers along it.

Tim was building a list of things he wanted to do. Wanted to try and explore and investigate. Which was interesting, he thought as he rinsed the washcloth one more time, since, until this morning, he'd never really given the idea of being with another guy a lot of thought. He'd never found the thought particularly distressing or anything. He'd just...been with women.

He was starting to appreciate why he got so many of those "you are such an idiot" looks.

Once he'd wrung out most of the water, he draped the cloth over the edge of the sink and put his hands back where they'd started—high on the tops of Chris's thighs. He dug his thumbs into the silky skin, and pushed.

"Spread 'em," he said, waggling his eyebrows.

Chris groaned. "That is not sexy," he complained, even as he did as he was told and opened his legs farther.

Tim ran his hands higher, gently brushing his thumbs against Chris's sac. "How's this, then?" Tim asked, his voice dropping to a deeper register, like it always did when he was really turned on.

Women seemed to like that. And Chris didn't seem unaffected either, though he was trying hard not to show it. "How's what? You haven't—"

Tim cupped Chris's balls in one hand, stroking his fingers along the thin skin, while his other hand pulled Chris's cock from his stomach and he curled his fingers around it. It was longer than his own. A little thinner and paler. And hot. Hotter than Tim had expected—and since he *had* a dick, he hadn't really thought there'd be any surprises.

"Better?" he asked, sliding his hand up the length of the shaft and listening to Chris suck in a deep breath.

"Fuck. Yes. *Yes.* But you don't have to. I know you haven't—"

"Shut up."

"Okay," Chris said, his entire torso jerking with his vehement nod. He looked wrecked. His hair stood on end from his own fingers, eyes bright and cheeks pink. It was a good look on him. A *really* good look.

Tim rose onto his knees and released Chris's balls to thread a hand into his hair instead. "Come here."

Chris tipped forward and met his lips, groaning as Tim's tongue slid into his mouth and twisted with his. Tim kept stroking the length of Chris's shaft, trying different things. Trying what he liked, then trying other stuff to see what Chris liked better, cataloging it all. Their lips parted only so Chris could let out desperate little gasps with each drag of Tim's hand.

The angle was weird, for both the kiss and the way he was holding Chris's cock, but only because it was the opposite from how he'd hold his own. So it was new, but also kind of great, he was learning, since this way he could run the pad of his thumb up the vein on the underside of Chris's shaft until he reached the frenulum, where he could then pause to swipe back and forth.

Chris squirmed against him, his good leg curling around Tim's hip, his calf digging into one of Tim's butt cheeks as he tried to drag him closer. Chris clutched at Tim's shoulder and the edge of the sink for dear life.

Their lips separated on another gasp from Chris. *"Fuck,* how are you so good at this?"

Tim hummed and kissed him again, pleased by the compliment. This was fresh territory and he was happy for the feedback. More than that, though, he *loved* making Chris feel good. Nothing got Tim hotter than getting someone else hot. And Chris...this was better than it had ever been before.

This man, who he'd loved as a friend for years, was panting for *him*. Was curling around him, and digging his fingers into his shoulders, and groaning, because *Tim* was doing these things to him.

The only thing Tim wanted to change—and he *would* change it—was how surprised Chris sounded, even as he was shuddering and gasping the word "fuck" helplessly with every pump of Tim's hand.

Tim wanted to make him *scream.*

He used the hand still buried in Chris's hair to push him

back, just a little, then ducked his head and sucked the very tip of Chris's cock into his mouth.

Chris did, in fact, scream through his orgasm. And thrash. And very nearly throw himself to the floor when the towel beneath him slipped precariously across the smooth porcelain surface, but Tim caught him in time.

"*Holy fuck*," Chris gasped once he'd caught his balance and his breath. "I can't believe you did that. I can't believe you *swallowed*."

Tim shrugged. "Why is that a big deal? I mean, other than the fact that we need to talk about how much coffee you've been drinking."

Chris appeared outraged. "Are you saying my semen tastes funny?"

"News flash, dude. Spunk tastes weird."

"Oh, I ah...wouldn't know?"

Tim sat back on his heels and looked up at Chris with surprise. "You wouldn't?"

"No. Why would I?"

"You're the one who just declared his big gay crush. Didn't you go out and find some guys to test this shit out on?"

"*No.* I'm not attracted to a lot of guys. And, for a while now, it's really just been...you know, *you*."

Which was really fucking awesome. Tim knew his smile was smug, based on Chris's disgruntled look alone.

He rose and captured Chris's lips and licked into his mouth, taking his time to kiss him thoroughly. When he finally leaned back, Chris made a face.

"You're right. That tastes weird."

"How have you never tasted your own, at least?"

"Eeww?"

"Don't you ever experiment?" Tim asked incredulously. Because, seriously, that's *all* Tim had been doing since the minute he discovered his dick.

"Is that what this is?" Chris asked quietly.

"What do you mean?"

"Is this an experiment? Are we experimenting?"

Tim sat back on his heels. "No? I mean, I don't think so. Is that what you want?"

"No."

"Sooo...what do you want?" Tim asked carefully, knowing how much the answer meant already. *Shit shit shit.* They should have had this talk *before* he blew his best friend. That would definitely have been the smarter thing to do.

"I want us. To be together."

Tim was pleased by how sure Chris sounded. But he still had to be certain they were on the same page here. "Like dating?"

Chris made a face. "That sounds like holding hands and going to the movies."

"So, you don't want to hold hands at the movies?" Tim asked to clarify.

"No, asshole. I *do* want to hold your fucking hand at the movies. I'm just saying that the word dating doesn't really fit what I'm hoping for here."

"Don't be bitchy," Tim admonished, trying to keep the smile off his face and failing. "I'm just trying to understand."

"I'm saying that dating doesn't seem to cover the fact that we live and work together, you know? Or that I've...uh...had a lot of feelings for a while now. But. Whatever. I know this is new to you. As long as it's not an experiment, we can figure out the rest later."

Chris tried to stand, but Tim pressed him back and ducked his head to force Chris to meet his eyes. "Okay."

"We'll figure it out?"

"No, we go all in."

Chris swallowed heavily. "Really?"

"Yes. But on one condition."

"What?" Chris asked warily.

"I am doomed to fuck this up if you don't tell me what you're thinking, okay? None of that you-being-reserved shit. You have to tell me if I do something wrong or right or weird or whatever. And then we're going to have to be fucking adults and talk about shit. Deal?"

"We're going to be adults, huh? I guess we're trying a lot of new things today."

"Fuck you. Just agree, already."

"Yeah. Okay."

"Promise."

"I promise. Now do we have to do pinky swears or something?"

Tim grinned. "You're such a tool." Then he leaned in and kissed Chris again before he could object.

From there, it was fair to say Tim got distracted. It wasn't until he felt Chris's hand snaking down between their bodies and towards Tim's shorts that he called a halt to the kiss.

"No orgasms for me. Game tonight," he said, hauling himself to his feet and swatting Chris on the thigh. "Up you get. You need to get in bed and elevate that leg."

Chris blinked up at him. "You don't orgasm on game days?" he asked incredulously.

"I don't come *before* a game. Got to keep my stamina up and it tends to wind me a little," he admitted, a bit sheepish at the end.

Still, he had no idea why that made Chris laugh so hard. It was just common sense. He let Chris have his fun, though, since it was the first time in a while he'd seen that big, happy smile on Chris's face and he liked it.

He always had, actually. Had spent hours trying to put it there in the past, and relished the warm, happy feeling it created in his own chest once he'd succeeded.

In hindsight, it was a little embarrassing to realize all the ways he'd been kind of a fucking idiot.

Chris sat propped up in his bed and listened to the mysterious sounds coming from the kitchen. He felt like he was having some kind of out-of-body experience. His limbs felt loose, his muscles lax, his head still spinning a little from a really outstanding orgasm, followed immediately by the dreaded "relationship talk" that had gone about a thousand times better than he would have hoped for in his wildest dreams.

Maybe that was what this was. Maybe this was what his wildest dreams actually felt like.

A loud crash, followed by some really colorful cursing, came from the kitchen.

"You doing okay in there, buddy?" Chris called in the most patronizing tone he could manage.

"Fuck off!"

Chris grinned. Yeah, his life was pretty fucking fantastic right now. Surreal, but fantastic.

Tim had tucked him into bed, naked, and made him promise to rest his leg while Tim made lunch. Chris eyed his dresser, just a few feet away and filled with perfectly serviceable pajamas. Of course, in order to put any of them on, he'd have to cut one leg off and figure out how to get them on by himself. He was pretty flexible, but that would definitely be a challenge. Underwear would be, too, for that matter.

He looked down at the sheets pooled in his lap, Tim's quilt among the comforter and sheets, and tried not to feel weird. He just wasn't a naked guy, normally. Then again, he also wasn't normally the kind of guy who made weird keening noises when he climaxed.

Tim was a terrible influence.

Movement by the door caught his eye and he looked up to find Tim staring at him.

"What?" Chris asked, feeling self-conscious.

"You look really good."

Chris's heart stumbled in his chest. "Weren't you straight, like, a minute ago?"

Chris had always sucked at taking a compliment.

Tim just chuckled and handed him his turkey sandwich and another smoothie. His favorite kind, of course. Tim, who was still only wearing his boxer briefs, climbed into bed with his own plate. They sat side-by-side and ate.

"Are you coming to the game tonight?" Tim asked when he'd set aside their plates.

"I'd like to, but I'm not sure how I'd get around. Also, I have no pants."

"You can borrow a pair of my sweats. They should be big enough to fit over the cast." It was true—Tim's thighs were gigantic. And then there was that ass... "If I can get you to the team box without you having to crutch too much, will you come?"

Chris eyed Tim suspiciously. "Is this going to humiliate me?"

"No!" Tim said with wide-eyed innocence.

Chris didn't believe him for a minute, but it was also clear Tim wanted him to go and Chris was weak in the face of that. "Okay."

Tim leaned over and pressed a quick kiss to his lips. "Great."

Chris was still blinking with surprise when Tim left the room to do the dishes. Apparently, Tim was taking to this "all in" thing even better than Chris.

Chapter Five

An hour before the game, Chris stood in the lobby just inside the players and staff entrance to the Moncton Arena and glared at Tim.

"What? I said I'd get you to your seat without a lot of crutching. This works, right?"

Callum Morrison, former NHL goalie and current owner of the Moncton Ice Cats, chuckled and patted the golf cart they used to lug around flats of water and other heavy cargo under the arena. "Come on, Chris. I promise to be gentle."

With a heavy sigh, Chris hopped to the passenger seat and suffered through Tim helping him sit, stowing his crutches in the back, and heaving his casted leg up to rest on the front of the cart.

"Thanks," he muttered. They both just waved him off.

"I'll see you in a minute upstairs."

Chris turned to look at Tim. "What? Why?" But Tim was already gone. Callum started the cart and steered them carefully down the long corridor that ran under the arena. "Do you have any idea what he has planned?"

"Nope," Callum said easily. "I'm just the chauffeur."

Callum stopped right next to the elevator and helped Chris get back on his crutches, then rode with him to the mezzanine.

Chris frowned. "Can the cart stay in the hallway down there?"

"Not for long, but I want to see whatever Tim has planned," Callum said cheerfully.

Chris groaned. "God help me. Would it be too much to hope he'll let me walk to the box without making a fuss?"

Callum just chuckled, the sound turning to full out laughter when the doors opened and revealed the entire team, all of them grinning, and each holding a Sharpie aloft.

"Tim said if we helped you to your seat, we could sign your cast," Alexei announced with a dangerous smirk.

Chris groaned, then yelped as his crutches were yanked from his hands and he was forced to put his arms around two sets of shoulders, while two more guys pulled his legs out from under him.

"Careful guys! We don't want to break him any more than he already is!" called Rupert, the team's manager and Callum's husband, from the back of the scrum of players.

Somehow, miraculously, they got Chris to his seat in one piece. Then the idiots attacked his cast, pens flying.

"Do *not* draw dicks on my cast, you assholes!" Chris cried, knowing it was futile.

Tim put a hand on his shoulder and squeezed. "I told them this cast was coming off in just a few days. You may not be fit for polite company in the meantime."

"Jesus Christ," Chris moaned. "What the hell is my doctor going to think?"

"That you're a hockey player?" suggested Rupert with a grin.

Chris rolled his eyes and barely resisted telling his manager to take a flying leap.

He didn't bother to control himself an hour later when he, Rupert, and Callum were alone in the box, and the happy couple was entertaining themselves by reading aloud the ridiculous filth scrawled across Chris's cast.

"I'm pretty impressed with Dave's artistic abilities," Rupert mused. "I didn't know it was possible to draw such a realistic penis on fiberglass. Especially with a Sharpie."

Chris couldn't remember the last time he'd looked forward to puck drop quite so much, and that was saying something.

The game was a good one, even if it sucked to have to watch it from up in the team's box. Everyone skated well—including their opponents—and play flew up and down the ice. The first period was winding down when the puck was shoveled back to the point where Tim was waiting. His one-timer blew through a seemingly impenetrable wall of players and right to the back of the net.

Chris roared with the rest of the crowd, wishing he could jump to his feet like everyone else. Tim turned, before his linemates could even hug him, and pointed right at Chris.

Chris was one hundred percent certain the goofy look on his face was as embarrassing as the painfully happy squeezing feeling around his heart. Though, Jesus Christ, how had it not occurred to Chris that Tim wouldn't be able to keep this under wraps for more than ten seconds? For fuck's sake, Tim didn't even know what the word discreet *meant*.

Rupert's and Callum's cheers turned to hoots of laughter as Chris's face burned hotter and hotter. He snuck a look at them, nervous. Not that they'd care about the gay thing, obviously. But maybe they wouldn't be as keen on the whole fraternization issue.

Neither of them appeared to be anything but delighted. Of course, they probably didn't know anything. And even if they did, it occurred to Chris that they were close friends with Alexei and Mike, so maybe this wasn't anything new anyway.

The game resumed, capturing everyone's attention again, thank Christ. Chris tugged his phone from his pocket and set up a reminder to call his mom. She already knew about his feelings for Tim, but he'd never hear the end of it if he didn't tell her what was going on before Tim did something so obvious, she'd be able to tell what was going on just by watching one of their games on TV.

The Ice Cats won, but by the time the final horn went off, Chris was fading fast. Maybe it had been a little too ambitious to come out for a game. Rupert and Callum seemed to recognize that, too, and carefully helped him to the elevator. As soon as they arrived downstairs, Callum ran for the cart while Rupert waited with him. Callum came roaring around the corner with not just the cart, but Tim riding shotgun.

Tim barely waited until they came to a stop before jumping out of his seat. "You look like hell," he said, helping Chris to the cart.

"Yeah, well, have you smelled yourself? You didn't even rinse off, did you?"

"Nah. I figured you needed to get home."

Chris didn't argue. He was in bad shape. Such bad shape, he passed out pretty much the moment he got in the car. The walk from the parking lot to their apartment was hell, but he did it on his own. Tim tried to convince him to let Tim carry him, but Chris threatened to tell everyone they knew that he'd once caught Tim watching My Little Pony on TV...and that he had drunkenly confessed that Pinkie Pie was his favorite.

Chris barely remembered getting into bed. He might have actually fallen asleep while he was still standing in the middle of the room, letting Tim strip him down. That was probably how he ended up stark naked, anyway.

He was well asleep when something woke him, disoriented for just a moment. Then he felt the press of warm skin along his back, a strong arm still damp from the shower curling around his waist.

"Shh...go back to sleep," whispered Tim, his lips pressed to Chris's neck.

Chris wriggled back, planting himself firmly in Tim's lap, and did just that.

Tim woke the next morning with Chris draped across his chest, the covers pulled up so high only the wild thatch of Chris's light blond hair was visible. Tim's fingers itched to touch the silky strands, but he didn't want to wake Chris just yet.

Not that it would be easy. Chris was out cold. He'd woken up in the middle of the night, fidgety and sore from sleeping in the same position too long, and frustrated by exhaustion and his pain meds wearing off. He hadn't been able to fall asleep again until Tim had forcibly rearranged them so that he could act as a full-body pillow for Chris.

His motives had been pure, but now he was awake, hungry, and hard. His dick was pressed up against the thigh Chris had draped over his hips.

He wriggled a little, just to test the waters, and found that he could slide out from under Chris relatively easily. Chris didn't stir at all, which made Tim feel guilty and kept him where he was. He'd been so excited to bring Chris to the rink and have the guys see him, to have him watch the game, he had maybe jumped the gun on getting Chris out of the house for some fun.

Today, though, they had nowhere they had to be. The team was leaving for a road trip tomorrow, and Coach had given them a day of rest before a grueling four games in six days. Sadly, Tim was bound to disappoint his coach, because while he fully intended to spend the day in bed, it wasn't to spend a lot of time doing anything that could be termed as "rest".

For now, though, he let himself snooze for a little while longer, enjoying vague images of what he had planned that day and tinkering with those ideas as he went. At some point, his hand began to trail up and down Chris's back, his fingers drawn to the divot of Chris's spine and the soft skin that gave just a little before firm muscle pushed back.

Chris woke by nuzzling his face into Tim's chest. Tim smiled down at the top of Chris's head, charmed despite himself, his hand still moving gently. It froze, though, when something wet and warm licked over his nipple.

He grunted, his nipple contracting sharply, a slow, warm pulse of blood coursing toward his cock. His smile, though, didn't waver. He probably looked like a complete idiot grinning at the ceiling, but he was too delighted. Apparently, he wasn't the only one with ideas about the best way to spend the day.

Tugging on the comforter, he drew it down just far enough to see Chris's face, his eyelashes fluttering against the light. "Mmph," Chris muttered, turning to shield his eyes from the light and to suck Tim's nipple between his lips.

Tim's breath left him with a hiss. He wasn't usually much of a nipple guy. Or he hadn't been, but then again, most women had sort of ignored them. It still wasn't particularly overwhelming, but it was a surprise to see Chris's pink lips against his skin. He thought that alone was heightening everything else, so that each gentle tug transferred itself down deeper into his body.

"Come here," Tim said, his voice rough from sleep and yelling on the ice last night.

Chris lifted his head and smiled sleepily at Tim before leaning up to press their lips together.

Morning breath wasn't great, but it didn't matter at all when compared to being able to kiss Chris. Why hadn't they done this a year ago? Three years ago? He forced back the idea that he had so much time to make up for, the regret of time lost, and focused instead on now. He was doing such a thorough job of it, of kissing Chris, he didn't notice the movement under the covers until deft fingers trailed down his belly and through the thick hair surrounding the base of his cock.

Chris ended the kiss, leaning back when Tim chased his lips for more.

"You don't have a game today," Chris observed. Tim was sure he'd never seen Chris smile like that before this morning. If he had, he might have figured shit out a whole lot faster—and reciprocated a lot sooner, too.

"I don't," he agreed, intrigued to see what Chris would do next.

Chris's eyes narrowed, studying him. Then his long, warm fingers curled around Tim's cock and tugged. It felt like a challenge. One Tim met by arching one eyebrow and smirking, because this was still *them* and he wasn't going to make it easy. What would be the fun in that?

Chris's narrow gaze never wavered as his fingers danced lightly up the length of Tim's shaft, smoothing over the head and back down again. Exploring.

Tim gritted his teeth, keeping his face impassive and choking back a groan when Chris's grip tightened. Tim broke, though, when even a hint of worry snuck onto Chris's face. He cupped his hands around Chris's jaw and captured his lips again.

"So good," he murmured against Chris's lip. "Please."

Chris nodded, their noses bumping, their lips and tongue

still tangled. Tim's breath went shaky, his hand slipping down Chris's back to his ass, anchoring him close.

It didn't take long. In fact, Tim considered being a little embarrassed about how quickly he got to the point of gasping, fingers knotted in Chris's hair and digging into his firm ass. Tim tipped his head back and shouted through his orgasm.

He floated for a moment, warm and happy and utterly content. He thought he could go back to sleep and Chris would forgive him. Would even understand. It was a nice feeling.

Tim wouldn't do that, of course. That kind of selfishness wasn't in his programming. He was perfectly aware of Chris's erection pressed to his hip and how hard Chris was trying not to squirm, based on how his glutes clenched and released under Tim's palm.

The moment Tim's head stopped swimming, he rolled Chris onto his back and climbed over him. "Tell me what you like," he said, then without waiting for a response, sucked Chris's cock as far into his mouth as he could without gagging himself.

"Oh, fucking Christ," Chris groaned, his knuckles going white around fistfuls of the flannel sheets.

Tim bobbed his head experimentally, trying to find a good rhythm and level of suction. It was actually really fucking hard to figure out what was best, since Chris was groaning and muttering through everything with roughly equal amounts of enthusiasm. Which was to say, a *lot.* Tim almost drew off just to ask if Chris could manage more detailed feedback, but one glance at Chris's face told Tim there would be no articulation from that quarter.

Chris's face was flushed pink, his eyes screwed closed as he gasped and squirmed. Tim put one hand on Chris's belly, and loved how it dipped and juddered with every shaky breath. Since Chris apparently wasn't going to be bothered much by whatever Tim did, he tried a few things. Taking Chris's cock deeper into his mouth triggered his gag reflex, but it also forced a punched-out breath from Chris, which Tim liked a lot. He tried it again, until his chin and Chris's cock were wet and messy with saliva and

Chris was swearing viciously. Tim tried everything, but kept coming back to trying to take Chris deeper. He did it while holding his breath, then while breathing in, breathing out, until he realized all he really needed was practice. It wasn't too long before his gag reflex started to give up on him.

That was so *cool.*

He pulled off Chris with an obscene noise and a swirl of his tongue. "Dude," he said breathlessly, "I'm totally going to be able to deep-throat you soon."

Chris's head popped up and he looked at Tim like he was insane, his eyes wild.

Tim dove back into his work, and Chris's head fell back to the mattress with a thump. From there, it didn't take long. Chris warned him with a hand in his hair, trying to yank him off, and Tim's dick perked up with interest with every pull.

Huh. Another thing to explore later.

"Fuck, Tim. *Tim.* You have to—I'm gonna—"

Tim's only response was to suck harder. Chris curled up, his abdominal muscles bunching in stark relief, and came with what Tim might generously call a high-pitched shout.

But would be sure to call a scream when he teased Chris about it later.

Chris collapsed back onto the bed, the hand that had been yanking at Tim's hair pushing at his head weakly when he became too sensitive.

Tim pulled back, curling his tongue around the soft head once, just to be tidy, and released Chris's cock from his lips.

Chris was staring at the ceiling blankly, his arms flung out the width of the mattress. His chest heaved as he sucked in great gulps of air, color slowly returning to normal. He looked wrecked. Again.

Tim felt accomplished.

He crawled up the bed and looked into Chris's glazed eyes. "You okay there, buddy?"

"Nngh." Chris's gaze drifted to him and held, and for a long moment, Tim got lost in just that. Chris's eyes were so blue. His lashes long, just a few shades darker than his hair, and slightly curled. Gorgeous.

Why hadn't he ever noticed that before?

If he'd had a mirror, he would have given *himself* the "you're such an idiot" look.

"You're pretty," he said with a little smile.

Chris blinked, his gaze narrowing. "Are you fucking with me?"

"No," he said, maybe a little dishonestly, since he could have chosen any number of other words—handsome, gorgeous, stunning—and not have needled Chris so much with it.

Chris shifted on the bed and grimaced.

"What? What is it? Did I hurt your leg?" Tim asked, sitting up quickly.

"No, no, my leg is fine. I ahh…"

Tim watched in fascination as a blush swept over Chris's face.

"What is it?" Tim asked again.

"I think there's a lot of…umm…spit? Down there? Between— beneath. You know."

Tim grinned and pecked Chris on the lips. He was sorely tempted to give Chris shit for being shy, but decided he enjoyed the idea of making a project out of teaching Chris to be uninhibited.

"I'll be right back," he promised with a last kiss.

Chris protested mightily when Tim returned with a warm washcloth and rolled Chris onto his stomach, nudging his thighs as wide apart as the cast would allow. Chris buried his bright red face in the sheets while Tim made quick work of wiping Chris down, forcing himself to remain detached when his innate curiosity was screaming at him to explore all the places he was seeing and touching for the first time.

If he gave into that, there wasn't a chance in hell either of them would get breakfast.

Tim threw the washcloth into the sink, coming back to find Chris's breathing had gone deep and soft, his eyes closed and his mouth lax. Tim pulled the covers up off the floor and tucked them in around Chris before padding out of the bedroom.

Chris woke slowly, his body melted into the bed, consciousness returning when the smell of coffee and cinnamon permeated his sleep-addled brain. He sat up, carefully dragging himself to sit against the headboard, barely settling before Tim came into the room.

"Is that french toast?" Chris asked incredulously.

It was. It was fucking *french toast.*

The surreal feeling was back. But it wasn't bad. Hell, no. Not when it came with cinnamon and butter and maple-flavored fucking awesomeness.

"Shut up and eat, loser," Tim said with a little smile as he climbed into bed beside Chris.

Chris did as he was told, but only because his mouth was too busy eating to tell Tim to fuck off. Tim, on the other hand, ate slowly. Chris kept catching Tim watching him out of the corner of his eye.

It was a little disconcerting, but also nice. The Tim he'd always known, the one he'd fallen in love with, was fun and funny. Gregarious and boisterous. Generous with his friends, with his time. But never so *attentive.*

Chris wondered what had gone wrong with all those women if this was how Tim treated them. Or maybe this was how Tim had learned to be, to make up for whatever shortcomings they saw in him.

"You know you don't have to feed me, right?" Chris said suddenly.

"I know," Tim agreed with an easy shrug.

"Even with the whole cast thing."

"Yup."

Chris tried to read Tim's face, but he was finally focused on his food. "I won't be mad if you don't. Or expect you to, now that we've...done stuff. You know that, right?"

"Considering I'm going to be gone for most of the next week, I should hope not."

Chris's heart sank. He'd been trying not to think about the road trip. "Oh, yeah. Right. It should be interesting, having to fend for myself," he said as brightly as he could. Tim shot him an amused, if somewhat insulting, look. "What? I'll be fine."

Tim rolled his eyes. "I've already talked to Callum. Rupert is on the road with us, but Callum's staying home with the kids and is happy to keep an eye on you. He's going to ask if you want to stay with them while we're gone."

Chris sputtered, simultaneously touched and put out that Tim had talked to them about this. "You didn't have to do that."

Tim finally put down his fork. Then his entire plate on the bedside table. Chris licked his lips nervously, not sure what was coming. He twitched when Tim took his hand and pulled into his lap.

"Look, I'm sorry if I've been pushy, okay? To be honest, you getting hurt kind of threw me for a loop."

"I'm sorry," Chris said.

"Shut up. It's not like you asked for this. But it has made me think a lot. About you. About us. Even before you told me everything yesterday and all this happened," he said, gesturing at the bed. "And what I've figured out is that I like taking care of you. I *want* to take care of you."

Chris looked back at Tim, bewildered. "You do? Why?"

Tim looked at him like he was an idiot. "Because I love you," he said, like it was perfectly obvious.

"You—you—what?" Chris spluttered when he could finally draw a proper breath.

"I love you. I mean, I've loved you for a long time. Like, years."

Oh. Right. "You mean like a friend."

"I did. I mean, I do? I don't know," Tim said with an

impatient sigh. "Look, I'm still figuring shit out, obviously, since it's been, like, two days. But I love you, okay? And that's been about friendship for a long time. But then you got hurt, and I've sucked your dick a couple times, and that's definitely changing things for me, you know?"

Chris really didn't, since he'd loved Tim in the dick-sucking way for a long time, but he nodded anyway, his heart galloping in his chest. "Okay," he said, though it came out somewhat strangled.

He felt like he should say it back—tell Tim he loved him, too. Tim made it sound so fucking easy, to just let the words past his lips. It *had* been easy yesterday when he'd been yelling at Tim, too caught up in the moment to engage any kind of filter. Now, though, with Tim's dark gaze looking directly into his, Chris realized Tim wasn't the only one struggling to get used to all the changes.

Chris had opened his mouth, even moved his lips to form the words, a few times, before Tim sighed again, this time with far more exasperation and a giant eye roll. "Don't hurt yourself, dude. We can take our time figuring things out." He plucked Chris's empty plate from his lap and put it aside.

Chris was still trying to wrap his head around what Tim had said, and now also the realization that, of the two of them, *Tim Robineau* was the one that was better at this relationship thing.

"Thanks," Chris said quietly, meeting Tim's steady gaze. "I'm sorry I'm being reserved again."

Tim smiled. "Well, I happen to know a way around that, now." He waggled his eyebrows.

Chris was mortified to feel himself blush furiously. "No you don't," he protested.

He leaned away from the wicked smile that stretched across Tim's face. "Wanna bet?"

Chris swallowed hard. The answer should be no. He should definitely *say no*.

Instead the words, "I dare you," came out of his mouth.

71

Chapter Six

Tim laughed, a sound so big and happy, Chris couldn't help but smile, too. That smile was erased, though, when Tim pounced on him, dragging his ass down the bed until he was flat on his back and Tim's wicked grin and big body were hovering above him.

"I'm going to fuck you," Tim announced in a deep voice.

Chris opened his mouth, to say god-only-knew what, but all that came out was a squeak.

"Is that a yes?" Tim asked, his eyes dancing with laughter.

"Fuck you," Chris groaned, hooking a hand around Tim's neck and tugging him closer, kissing him hard, trying to find some way of saying, "Yes, please, and hurry the fuck up" without actually having to speak the words.

Tim kissed like he played hockey, with focus and energy, using his strength to move his opponents out of the way. Or in this case, move Chris right where he wanted him, cast and all. Chris held on for dear life, his head spinning while Tim nipped at his lips, then dragged his mouth down Chris's neck and behind his ear, finding a spot that made Chris whimper helplessly. Tim's hands were everywhere.

Goddamn, Tim was good at this. Chris felt like a rookie by comparison.

"You're not built like a rookie," Tim said, a wealth of appreciation in his voice as he ran his hands down Chris's flanks.

Chris blinked, realizing he must have spoken aloud. God, he hoped he hadn't babbled all of that. He was reassured by the knowledge that his tongue had been too busy trying to wrap around Tim's for a good portion of the last five minutes.

"Uh, thanks," he said awkwardly, gulping when Tim pressed his legs wider on the bed so he could kneel between them.

"You're welcome," Tim murmured, running his eyes down

Chris's torso, lingering where his erection rested against his hip.

Chris jumped when Tim wrapped a hand around his cock.

"I bet this would feel great inside me," Tim said contemplatively.

All the air left Chris's lungs in a rush, his mouth hanging open.

Tim smirked. "Not going to agree? I think you should agree," he said. His hand hadn't stopped moving.

How the hell was Chris supposed to *speak* when he wanted to die of lust *and* embarrassment?

"Yes," he finally managed to hiss out. "Yes. I want that. *Please.*"

"We can't," Tim said sadly.

Chris pushed up onto his elbows. "*What?* Why'd you even say it if you don't want—"

"Oh, I do want," Tim promised while his thumb did honestly mind-blowing things around the head of Chris's cock. "But I can't. Not with all the games this week. But later. When I get back and have two days off…"

Chris let his head fall back between his shoulders and tried to breath. "Fuck. *Tim.* You're killing me."

"Sorry."

He didn't sound sorry. Not even a little. Then Chris had a thought. It took an absurd amount of energy to lift his head again, but he wanted to see Tim when he said, "You know, you might not like it. And that's cool."

"Don't worry. I'm going to like it."

"How do you know?" And suddenly, Chris was afraid to know the answer. "Have you…you've been with a man? Before?"

"Nope," Tim said easily, his lips popping on the P.

"Then you don't know," Chris said, trying to ignore the relief surging through him. It shouldn't make a difference that he was the only man Tim had even been with.

"Alison," Tim said, dropping his ex-girlfriend's name into the conversation out of nowhere.

Chris focused back on Tim, shaking his head in confusion. Then it clicked, a shudder running through Chris's body as the most insane images burned themselves into his head. "Are you fucking kidding me? You. And she. You let her..."

"Peg me? Yep." Another popped P, another stroke along Chris's cock.

"You know, being smug about it is *not* attractive. Like, at all." To utterly belie that point, Tim's finger caught the pearl of precome on the tip of Chris's dick and rubbed it into his skin. "*Fuck*," Chris groaned, his good leg twitching against the sheets.

"That good?" Tim asked mildly, his hand speeding up.

"Yes, you bastard," Chris gasped as he writhed helplessly. "Yes, it's fucking good."

"Good," Tim murmured, bending to return his mouth to Chris's neck, his shoulders, his lips tracking all over Chris's chest and torso.

Chris ran his fingers through Tim's hair. He'd fucking *known* it would feel like this. Soft and thick. Like mink fur. He ran his other hand over Tim's shoulder, along his jaw where the stubble scraped gently against his fingertips.

"You know, I'm not going to just lie here when I'm not in this cast anymore," Chris promised, cutting himself off with a gasping giggle as gentle fingers danced over his ribs. He was helpless to whatever Tim wanted to do, and Tim was shamelessly taking advantage of it. And *fuck fuck fuck*, why was that so hot?

Tim's lips brushed Chris's pec when he replied. "I look forward to it."

Chris groaned, his cock leaking again. "Please, god, do something. I swear my balls must be blue by now."

He jerked, hard, when Tim cradled his sac gently in his palm.

"Nope, they look fine," he said sweetly.

"Uuugh," Chris groaned, wishing he could cut the fucking cast off right now. It would be worth it, just so he could wrap his legs around Tim's waist, pull him close, feel his ribs against the sensitive skin of his thighs. His good leg actually lifted off the bed at the thought—the bad leg, too, barely, but Tim pushed it down.

"Careful," Tim admonished before he dipped his tongue into Chris's belly button, twice, then sat back on his heels.

"Here," Tim said, shoving a few pillows under the cast, pushing it as wide as Chris's hips would allow. "Better?"

It was, actually. Chris didn't have time to tell Tim as much, though, before Tim was leaning over him and digging through the bedside table drawer.

"Hey," Chris protested, racking his brain to recall if he had any decent lube in there. He blinked when Tim came back with a bottle he'd never seen before. "Where did that come from?"

"My room?" Tim replied with a little smile.

"Fucking boy scout," Chris groused, trying to look put out, which wasn't easy when his heart was banging against his ribs so hard he was sure the whole city could hear it. He watched in a daze as Tim poured some into his palm, letting it warm there briefly before wrapping his hand around Chris's cock again.

He hissed at the sweet, slick slide. His body felt hot, flushed all over, a bead of sweat trickling down his temple. Tim seemed to know exactly how much pressure to use to drive him fucking crazy without taking him to the edge.

His heart stuttered in his chest when Tim's other hand disappeared between his legs.

"I've never done this before," Chris blurted, the flush in his cheeks instantly turning to fire.

Tim froze, his eyes snapping up to Chris's face, which, remarkably, *could* burn hotter, apparently.

"With anyone?" Tim asked.

"Um...no? I mean, I've had sex with women. A while ago, I guess. Before I realized I—you..." Chris sighed, annoyed with himself now for not being able to get the words out. He steeled himself to at least be able to give the answer to Tim's question. "But no, not, you know." He gestured vaguely between them. So much for using his words.

"Not anal sex?" Tim asked, and there was no judgement in his tone, just the sense that he was looking for clarity. Which was good, Chris thought, trying to control his breathing and his blush.

"No. No pegging either, you fucking over-achiever."

Tim grinned and something inside Chris loosened.

"Good," Tim said.

"I thought you said I should experiment," Chris shot back, just to be contrary.

"That was before I knew I wanted to be the only one," Tim replied with a little self-deprecating shrug.

And, *oh.* That was...Chris sat up, cupped Tim's jaw, and drew him into a kiss. Tim immediately bullied his way into Chris's mouth, of course, taking control, but Chris wasn't going to pretend he didn't like it. When their lips separated for a second, Chris whispered, "Me, too."

Tim's hand tightened around Chris's cock, making him moan. "Good," Tim said again. "I'm going to stretch you open now," he announced, circling a slick finger around Chris's hole.

Every muscle in Chris's body tightened up. "Okay."

Tim rolled his eyes fondly and pushed him back onto the bed. "Hold on."

Hold on? Hold on to what? Hold on *for* what?

The press of Tim's finger seemed like an answer to that, and Chris squirmed, forcing his cock up into Tim's hand, then pushing back against that finger. It slipped in easily, and Chris let out a long, shuddering breath.

That was...not bad. Kind of good, actually. Especially when Tim started moving, dragging his knuckle past Chris's rim, then thrusting back in, farther each time. He added more lube, and it felt messy in all sorts of good and filthy ways.

A moan escaped Chris's throat unbidden.

"God, I wish you could see yourself," Tim murmured.

Chris squirmed under his gaze, but couldn't find any words.

"You're fucking gorgeous like this," Tim added, distracting

Chris from the gentle prodding of a second finger along his rim.

Chris opened his mouth to say something, possibly "shut up", when that second finger slipped in. His mouth snapped closed.

That was...interesting. The muscles that had given so easily for one finger were resisting the second. Still not bad. It didn't hurt. But there was definitely a stretch. Chris wriggled a little when Tim added more lube directly from the bottle, then pushed his fingers in farther.

"Oh," Chris gasped. "That's—yeah, that's good."

Tim pumped his fist over Chris's cock, taking up a steady stroke in counterpoint to what his fingers were doing inside Chris. A rush of heat worked through Chris from those two points of contact, loosening every muscle. Tim's fingers were going deeper each time. Then he crooked his fingers, and pleasure burst over Chris's entire body. He jerked like he'd been electrified.

"Holy shit. What was that? Fuck. Fuck," Chris babbled as Tim mastered the art of nailing that spot with every thrust.

Tim grinned down at him and hit it again. "That's your prostate."

"*Fuck.* Don't stop. Please, Tim. Don't ever stop."

Tim's chuckle was warm and washed over Chris. "Okay, sweetheart. I won't stop."

And he didn't. He just kept doing it, and Chris just kept *talking*. It was horrible and wonderful and he never wanted it to stop, but please god, why wouldn't he just *shut up*?

He was in the midst of a veritable tirade about how magical Tim was when Tim tucked a third finger in and pressed deep, until the pad of his finger was pinned to that spot and Chris's rim was stretched wide.

Chris's words cut off with a deep, happy groan. "*Fuuuuuck,*" he sighed. He curled his arm around Tim's shoulders when Tim pressed his lips right over Chris's heart, not caring how it made the angle of Tim's fingers weird or squashed his dick in Tim's fist between their bodies. He thought he could stay like this forever.

He told Tim as much. Told him he was gorgeous and had the best hands, both on the ice and in bed. He told Tim how he'd jerked off thinking about doing this, but hadn't imagined it right at all. That this was better. *Tim* was better than he ever fantasized. And how he never, ever wanted to stop doing this. With Tim.

Tim started out laughing at the stream of confessions pouring from Chris's lips, but by the end, he was flushed and sweating, his shoulders trembling beneath Chris's hands.

His voice was rough when he gasped, "Chris. *Chris*, I can't wait anymore, okay? *Please.*"

Chris pressed a hand to Tim's cheek and forced him to lift his head. He ran his fingers along Tim's jaw, the pads catching on the stubble there, and smiled. "I want you to fuck me now. Please."

Tim jerked forward and kissed him fiercely, and then just as quickly pulled away to settle on his heels between Chris's legs. Tim's eyes turned calculating, and Chris's heart thumped heavily in his chest as he watched Tim dump an obscene amount of lube over his bare dick.

Tim looked up. "Is this okay?"

Chris didn't have to ask if Tim was clean. He knew he was, and not just because the team got them all tested. But also because they actually *did* talk about that shit. That was how he knew Tim had never gone bare before. And Tim knew Chris hadn't either.

"Yes."

Tim's breath left him with a huff, a smile flashing over his face before he proceeded to attack Chris with the sheets.

"What the fuck are you doing?" Chris squawked, as Tim wrapped his cast in flannel and summarily rolled Chris onto that side. His next protest left him with a gasp when Tim slide up behind him, cupping the back of his good leg and bringing it up to his chest.

"Here. Hold this."

"What?" Chris asked blankly, hooking his hand behind his knee as instructed.

"Fucking cast," Tim muttered as he plastered himself to Chris's back. "Is this okay?"

Chris nodded frantically, his brain finally catching up with what was happening. He was acutely aware of the slide of Tim's cock along his spine as Tim eased further down the bed, until his chin was hooked over Chris's shoulder and he settled on the mattress.

Chris whimpered when Tim's fingers slid back into his ass, testing his rim. "God, you feel so fucking good. So tight," Tim said, his lips brushing Chris's ear. Then his fingers were gone, and Chris held his breath as the broad head of Tim's cock pressed up against him.

Tim's other arm curled under Chris's neck and over his chest, holding him close.

"You sure?"

Chris looked up into Tim's eyes, so close. "Of course I'm sure. I love you."

Why were those words ever hard to say?

Tim's hold tightened, crushing Chris against him. "I love you, too," he said, his voice hoarse. Then his hips pressed forward, and the joy rushing through Chris was tangled with the slow, hot stretch of his body opening to Tim, the burn unlike anything he'd experienced in his life.

He tested his body all the time. It was his job. But this was a measure he had never taken, and it felt good. Letting the tension go and feeling Tim push past his rim, taking Tim into his body, felt fucking amazing.

Tim trembled behind him, moving his hips in gentle waves that pushed him farther into Chris. Brought them closer. Chris grabbed the hand on his chest, pressing it over his heart and wriggled back.

Because, seriously, this was taking too long.

Tim groaned against Chris's shoulder. "What are you *doing*?"

Chris shifted back again. "I'm trying to get you to fuck me," he said with a frustrated sigh.

Tim's head popped up and his hips jerked forward, forcing his cock deeper.

Chris whimpered, his eyes fluttering shut.

"I was trying to be all romantic and slow and shit," Tim confessed.

"Knock it off."

"But—"

"You can romance the shit out of me another time. I swear. Just please, please, now I want you to *move*."

Tim chuckled, the sound buzzing directly from his chest through Chris's back. His lips traced over Chris's shoulder. "Okay, then."

Tim's hips rolled forward, and Chris pushed back, gasping as his body felt split in two by the long, hard thrust of Tim's cock taking up residence deep inside him. *Fuck.* Tim's hips pressed against his ass and he ground up against Chris, stretching him wider.

"Like that?" Tim asked.

Chris nodded frantically. His heart galloped in his chest. It felt amazing. He got why some people would say it hurt, but Chris was a hockey player, and he knew that some hurts were the *good* kind.

Tim shifted against him again and on the next grind, hit that fucking *spot*.

"Oh, fuck. *Tim.* Please," Chris gasped, turning his face to bury it against the sheet.

He groaned when Tim eased back, every inch of his shaft easing from Chris's body and dragging over his rim sending bolts of pleasure through Chris. Chris's mouth hung open, ready to beg, when Tim thrust back in.

A grunt burst from Chris's throat when Tim glanced over that sweet spot then bottomed out.

Tim laughed and groaned at the same time.

"What?" Chris asked, practically delirious with pleasure, but not so far gone he didn't know Tim was laughing at him.

"That's the exact sound you make when you're on the bench press."

To prove his point, Tim thrust again and another grunt tore from Chris. It was a good sound. Chris was too busy trying to process the deluge of sensations currently roaring through his body to come up with a better riposte than, "*Shut up.* You like it."

"Yeah. I do," Tim replied, and Chris could *hear* his smile. Then Tim started working his hips in earnest, never letting up, and Chris made the noise again, over and over.

As some point, the burn was replaced with pure pleasure. The stretch lost to overwhelming need. It all felt so fucking good. Tim thrust harder, faster, forcing that damn noise up and out of Chris time and again, and Chris didn't care. Well, he did care. Because he never wanted this to end. He never wanted to stop making ridiculous noises if it meant Tim would fuck him like this, hold him close and whisper obscene promises in his ear and bury his cock so deep into Chris's body he couldn't tell where one of them ended and the other began.

He jumped when Tim's hand curled around his cock, so that each thrust pushed Chris's dick through his fist. Chris would have bruises on his ribs where Tim's other hand anchored him, held him fast against each punch of Tim's hips.

"Fuck, Fuck," Tim chanted against Chris's shoulder, eventually gasping, "I'm close."

He slammed forward one more time and ground his hips, his hand flying over Chris's cock. Chris's back arched, the building tension pulling taut until only his shoulders and his ass were touching Tim and he was grinding back.

His climax crashed over him like a Zamboni going highway speed. The world went white, his only anchor to reality the press of Tim's hands and the heavy press of his cock.

Sensation returned with a rush, though Chris had no idea how much later. A second? An hour? It started with the hot bite of Tim's teeth against his shoulder, and the loud, almost painful-sounding groan in his ear.

Chris reached behind him as best he could and held Tim

close as he shook through his orgasm, his other hand stilling Tim's on his over-sensitive cock.

Tim slumped onto the bed and against him. "Holy shit," he whispered.

Chris chuckled, then winced as Tim's cock began to slip from his body. Tim's hand patted his hip, as if in apology, a moment before he pulled the rest of the way out. Chris winced, but mostly from how sensitive he was, not because of any pain.

He expected Tim to go get something to clean them up, but instead he just scooted back enough to help Chris roll onto his back, then curled back around him, tucking his legs so that Chris had to drape his good leg over them.

Chris stared up at the ceiling, very, very aware of his ass leaking onto the sheets, and possibly onto Tim. It was mind-bendingly hot, when by all rights it should have been the opposite. Hell, they were both *covered* in lube and come, and Chris didn't want to move a muscle to change it.

Tim hummed and slid a hand down past Chris's cock and behind his balls. Chris was too fucked out to flinch, not even when Tim pressed two fingers back inside his hole.

"What are you doing?" he asked curiously.

"Afterglow," came Tim's slurred response.

"Isn't this kind of messy for you?"

"Exceptions should be made."

Chris grinned, then turned to look at Tim's face.

Tim blinked back blearily.

"I've been in love with you for a long time," Chris confessed quietly. "I'm sorry I didn't tell you. I just...I never thought you'd feel the same, you know? But I promise I'll be better. I'll tell you things."

Tim patted Chris's stomach gently, a slow smile stretching across his face. "It's okay, baby. I know how to get you to talk now."

About the Author

Samantha Wayland has three great loves in life; her family, writing books, and hockey. She is often found apologizing to the first for how much time and attention is taken up by the latter two, but they forgive her because they are awesome and she clearly doesn't deserve them.

Sam lives with her family—of both the two and four-legged variety—outside of Boston. She is a wicked passionate New Englander (born and raised) who has been known to wax rhapsodic about the Maine Coast, the mountains of New Hampshire and Vermont, and the sensible way in which her local brethren don't see a need for directional signals (blinkahs!). When she's not locked away in her home office, she can generally be found tucked in the corner of the local Thai place with other socially-starved authors and an adult beverage.

Her favorite things include mango martinis, tiny Chihuahuas with big attitude problems, and the Oxford comma.

Sam loves to hear from readers. Email her at samantha@samanthawayland.com or find her on Facebook or Twitter (@samwayland).

Also by Samantha Wayland

With Grace

A man yearning to explore his sexual tastes but afraid to turn up the heat, the woman who loves him but is hungry for more spice...and the chef who craves them both.

When Grace, Philip and Mark find a mobster's flash drive full of incriminating information, they are quickly embroiled in a dangerous situation. They stay together for safety, but proximity ignites the sparks they've long been fighting to ignore.

When three friends dare to succumb to their appetites, they find the perfect recipe for love.

Destiny Calls

Patrick didn't think it would be a big deal to kiss Brandon, his best friend and fellow police officer. Hell, they'd done crazier things to escape a bar fight. But then he had no way of knowing just how hot it would be.

Destiny Matthews is not a woman who is afraid to ask for what she wants, and when she sees her two best friends kissing, she knows just what she's going to ask for. Before she can convince Patrick that he's not as straight as he likes to protest, Brandon is attacked by an unknown enemy.

While they fight to protect each other's lives, they prove time and again that they're even better at protecting their own hearts.

Fair Play

Hat Trick Book One

Savannah Morrison is the new athletic trainer for the Moncton Ice Cats, a professional hockey team in the wilds of New Brunswick. It's a good thing she's got plenty of knowledge and grit, because as the only woman trainer in the league, she has to work twice as hard to win the players' respect. The last thing on earth she would do is date one of them.

Twelve year hockey veteran Garrick LeBlanc isn't ready to hang up his skates, particularly since he hasn't figured out what the hell he's planning to do next. He needs the new trainer to keep him fit to play, and she's got the skills to do it. Too bad he lost his mind and hit on her the day they met. Now she hates his guts and he's made an art of ignoring her.

When the team is put up for sale, Garrick and Savannah have to work together to save their jobs and their team. Somewhere along the way, they discover Garrick isn't just a hockey player, Savannah isn't only passionate about her work, and just maybe they've got more in common than they thought.

Two Man Advantage
Hat Trick Book Two

Rhian is working his way up the ranks of professional hockey, with the dream of making it to the NHL getting closer every day. He's doing it alone—no family, no friends—and that's the way he likes it. Then he arrives in New Brunswick, and meets the Moncton Ice Cats. Suddenly, he's got friends—and even something that might be an honest-to-god crush.

Garrick is lonely and counting the days until his last season with the Ice Cats is over and he can move to Boston. When his girlfriend suggests he take a lover—as long that lover is a man and Garrick tells her all about it—he laughs it off. But damned if his buddy Rhian doesn't take on the starring role in his fantasies. Good thing Rhian is way too young—and straight—for what Garrick has in mind.

Rhian takes a chance when Garrick's increasingly confusing signals start making sense, and soon discovers he's bitten off more than he can chew. Sex with strangers is simple. Sex with his best friend? Complicated.

End Game
Hat Trick Book Three

Garrick LeBlanc never intended to fall in love with two people, but he has, and now he has to figure out what to do about it. He wants to make them happy, but is afraid he's doing just the opposite. To make matters worse, he's trapped in New Brunswick until the end of the hockey season, while his lovers are both in Boston.

Savannah Morrison has no one but herself to blame for practically shoving her lover into the arms of another man. After all, it was her idea that Garrick take a lover while they are separated for the season. She loves Garrick with all her heart, but how the hell is she going to share him with Rhian?

Rhian Savage used to have such a simple life. Now he's in love, his dreams of skating on an NHL team are coming true, and he keeps spotting a strangely familiar face in the crowds. To top it all off, he has to see Savannah every day. He knows she's Garrick's real future, but he doesn't have the balls to do the right thing for all of them and end it—until his life goes sideways. As usual.

Now Rhian is alone, Garrick is heartbroken, and Savannah— the one person Rhian figured would celebrate his departure—is beating down his door. What the hell is up with that?

Crashing the Net

Mike comes to Moncton wanting nothing more than to play for the Ice Cats and finally live on his own terms. He's broke, bruised, and covered from head to toe in cheap lube, but he isn't going to let that stop him. All he needs is a place to live and some time to figure out how to reconcile who he really is with who everyone wants him to be.

Dumping three gallons of lube on the new kid is just another day at the office for Alexei. He knows exactly who he is: a goalie on the ice, a prankster in the locker room, and a man who knows better than to share his private life with anyone. He's let people in before and it's taught him that if he can't have what he really wants, it's better to be alone.

Despite their apparent differences, an unlikely friendship grows. Neither of them could ever have guessed how much they *really* have in common.

Home & Away

You can build a team, but you have to find your home.

Rupert Smythe is fond of many things. Callum Morrison isn't one of them.

Rupert is a quiet, thoughtful business man and, sadly, a total wimp. Maybe not the ideal candidate to run a professional hockey team, but he signed on to do it anyway. As his life has reminded him on an almost daily basis since, this isn't the most brilliant idea he's ever had. And that was before Callum showed up.

Being in the spotlight is just part of being a professional athlete, but Callum needs a break. He arrives in Moncton unannounced, determined to help grow the team he just bought, and under the assumption he'd be welcome. Possibly he should have tried to make a better first impression.

Callum figures he can push through the rest of the summer, never expecting two kids, a host of friends, and his growing feelings for Rupert to derail everything he has ever believed about what he wanted, and what he could have.

Out of Her League

Lachlan Morrison's family likes to tell people that he's shy, but that's like saying the sky is sort of blue, or good hockey is just a little bit rough. Lachlan knows perfectly well he's a social disaster and works hard to humiliate himself as infrequently as possible.

Then Michaela Price, the most beautiful woman he's ever laid eyes on, moves to town, and she needs a friend.

Michaela knows she's no prize. As a nationally-known disgrace, she's pretty used to being stared at and having to chase photographers off the neighbors' roofs. She wouldn't wish her life on anyone, and certainly has no intention of inflicting herself on poor Lachlan Morrison, who literally cannot speak in her presence.

But then, going back to school isn't what she expected. It turns out her new life is just as lonely as the old version, and she only knows one person in town.

Checking It Twice

After four years with Alexei, there are a few things Mike knows with absolute certainty: he loves Alexei, Alexei loves him, and Alexei gives the very best gifts. This Christmas is no exception, though Mike is having a hell of a time figuring out what, exactly, Alexei's gift is.

Alexei knows his gift this year is going to blow Mike's mind, but in the meantime, it's pretty hilarious watching Mike try to figure out what it is. Granted, Alexei does have a lot of surprises in store for Mike this week, and it sure as hell isn't frankincense and myrrh.

A Merry Little (Hat Trick) Christmas

Hat Trick Book Four

'Tis the season to be jolly

Something is bothering Rhian, and his friends and family want to know what that is. His lovers, Garrick and Savannah, think they have an idea and they're trying to give him some space. His teammates haven't any clue, but they're convinced that enough nights out and beautiful women making eyes at him will make it better. And his grandfather and sister just want him to be happy and to know that he is loved.

Rhian Savage does know he's loved. He just wishes everyone else knew it, too.

Breaking Out

Mati Viveiros is done with men. Her family will never love her for who she really is, and the men she's dated haven't done much better. The only exception is Reese, who is the perfect boss, mentor, and friend. Wanting more would just be greedy.

Reese Lamont is finally in a place where he's genuinely satisfied with his life, his struggles in the past. Are there still things he wants? Sure, but he's too old to change his ways and he's never going to cast himself in the role of sleazy boss, so Mati can't ever know the extent of his feelings.

David Zapetti spent ten years with the Boston PD before realizing a change was required. Now he's in the personal protection business, where the money is good and the boredom immense, which is just what he wants. David knows the minute he sees Reese and Mati that there is nothing boring about either of them, but that doesn't stop him from volunteering to be their protection—and a whole lot more than that.

Printed in Great Britain
by Amazon

33158439R00057